I0818312

DO NOT MISS ALAN DALE DICKINSON'S

PREVIOUSLY PUBLISHED CRIME-FICTION MYSTERIES:

Charlie O'Brien, Private Investigator

Kidnap Country

The Money Changer

For the Love of Money

Charlie's Private Eye Angels

Orange County (California) Confidential

Baghdad Confidential

A Mystery in Laguna Woods

A Theft in Laguna Woods

A Kidnapping in Laguna Woods

The City of Brotherly Love

In addition, a published short primer on:

How to Write (and publish) a Novel

A Shooting in Laguna Woods

A CHARLIE O'BRIEN PRIVATE INVESTIGATOR MYSTERY

A Shooting in Laguna Woods

A CHARLIE O'BRIEN PRIVATE INVESTIGATOR MYSTERY

BY PROFESSOR
ALAN DALE DICKINSON

ISBN: 978-1-7326283-6-6

DICKINSON PUBLISHING COMPANY
PROFESSOR ALAN DALEDICKINSON
Chairman and Chief Executive Officer

Bank of America
Vice President and Business Banking Manager (Retired)
World Corporate Lending Group
P.O. Box 3962
Laguna Hills, CA 9265

A NOTE TO MY LOYAL READERS

As a self-admitted novice writer, albeit, internationally known mystery novelist, I try as hard as humanly possible to be as factual in my suspense novellas as I can be.

In order for this subject author to make this said mystery story lines as interesting, provocative, suspenseful and exciting as possible, I have taken some artistic and literary license here and there throughout this short story.

You might even say, if you would so desire, I have taken a lot of license and liberties. And these licensees include, however, are not limited to, places, objects, characters, guns, knives, players, names, and even possibly times and or dates.

Also, I shall be honest with you good readers, particularly those of you are experts in the "Kings English," that you may, just may, find a grammar and spelling error or some other writer 'faux-pas' in my little suspense thriller.

And, you may also note that some of the mysteries information, characters, and/or physical locations which are quite similar to those in real life are just a coincident and are not to be considered literary as such. This is a '*Fiction*' novel, period.

I trust that my loyal readers whom love mysteries as much as I do, will kindly overlook those small (and/or larger) mistakes and anomalies, and just sit back and enjoy the wild ride.

DEDICATION

To the good men and women deputies of the OCSD (Orange County Sheriff's Department), the excellent and newly elected, Don Barnes, Sheriff and Chief Coroner, Robert 'Bob' Peterson (Under Sheriff), and, the outstanding, Sergeant J. J. Hernandez (Community Safety Projects).

Captain Danks of the quite important Community Policing Department in Santa Ana, California. And, the great men and women officers of the BPD (Brea Police Department). Also, Captain Jeffrey Puckett, in charge of the Southwest Division of the OCSD.

In addition, the outstanding and dedicated BPD Police Chief, as well as Captain David Alan Dickinson, who is one of the finest and bravest police officers in all of Orange County.

The OCDA (Orange County District Attorney) Todd Spitzer, as well as all of the men and women who diligently serve in the OCDA's office.

And last however, clearly not least, to all of the 'Law Enforcement Agency' officers in Orange County whom risk their 'life

and limbs' on a daily basis, and also so bravely serve and protect the good citizens of the OC (Orange County) California.

To Howard Crawford, who taught me how to take a manuscript and go through all of the hundreds of steps, to get it ready for publishing on Amazon and Kindle eBooks. Both of which are two of the best and most professional Companies in the World.

David Alan, Desiree', Morgan and Scott, and, Mark Alan and Ramona. Jan (sister) a talented poet, and John, and their cool 'Cats.' Lisa (sister) a highly intelligent and strong woman, and Bob, and their two neat rescue dogs (Phoebe and Boomer).

Jan Smoker, a very loyal fan of 'Charlie' the PI, and a wonderful woman (mother-in-law). She has been extremely helpful with advice on Charlie's "Laguna Woods Mystery 'Trilogy."

Monja, Tammy and Richard of the fabulous 'Laguna Café' in Laguna Woods. They have great service, great food at very fair prices, as well as great smiles. I highly recommend it to my readers who live in South Orange County.

My dear and long-time friends, Thomas and Pamela, Don Kutz, Patrick, Irene, Janet, Tim, Ray and Judy, Pat, Diane, Ollie, Judy L., Sue and Mary Lou and Wayne Miller. The best G.P. doctor in all of Orange County, Dr. Anne, and the best D.C. in the OC, doctor Brett (and his wonderful fiancée', Bailey). Santa, and Sierra, and Angie, too.

My terrific U.S. bankers, John Kearney (Regional Manager), Jason, Christine, Nolan, Jackson and Iver. And also, to my two other great bankers, Mahmoud Alaeddin and Haroon Amini.

Also, last however certainly not least, our great neighbors, who are some of the best neighbors in all of Laguna Woods Village. Jim and Betty (big mystery fans), Krista and Kudta, Carol, Jo Nell, Peter and Grace, Cliff, Danny (a really great guy) and his nice wife, Hope (a E.R. Nurse).

SPECIAL DEDICATION

To Lynn, my lovely bride. You are my sole reason for living, as well as my inspiration for writing.

CHAPTER ONE

CHARLIE'S ALWAYS PRESENT cell phone rang in the middle of the night. It was about 2:00 am and he was sound asleep, cutting logs and snoring loudly, very loudly, when he was awakened by his ring-tone song, '*Private Eyes*' by the terrific 1980's pop duo, 'Hall and Oates' (John Oates and Daryl Hall).

Charles 'Charlie' Warner Kennedy O'Brien is one of only a few *trustworthy* PI's Private Investigators (or Private Detectives) in the United States or the whole world for that matter. He believes that people are put into jobs that they are gifted for. And he feels that he can do a lot of things well, however, he is really, really good at catching the 'bad guys.'

He *prays* every morning for protection from any harm during the day and meditates regularly during the day for wisdom in helping him to solve the crimes he is investigating, and then before he falls asleep at night, which is usually quite late, he thanks Dios for getting him safely though another day.

His ringtone is somewhat ironic and also funny to him as he is an *actual* PI (Private Investigator) in real life. Also, he really likes that great music team of 'Hall and Oates' and all of their many number one hits.

By the way, just in case you are interested in classic pop and rock music genre', that very popular tune was written by Warren Pash, Janna Allen, Sara Allen, and Daryl Hall. And it was released on September 1, 1981, do you recall where you were when you first heard that song? Charlie says that he does not, for some reason?

Charlie loves classic old rock-n-roll, Mo-Town, Do-wop, and Chicago Blues music, however, his favorite is Mo-Town, of course, he likes to call it, "Music-with Soul."

Charlie was having a wonderful dream and it was in living color. He was 'slow' dancing with his tall, exquisite and quite lovely wife, Lynn. She is the most intelligent woman that he has ever met and she also assists him with his private investigations.

The unwelcome and sleep-interrupting caller was *Sergeant J. J. Hernandez* from the OCSD (Orange County Sheriff's Department). Charlie just calls him "Sarge" and he is a great law enforcement officer by any means. He was a good friend of Charlie's and they had worked on, and solved, several criminal cases together in the OC (Orange County), California.

Sergeant Hernandez, and his two very capable supervisors, LT (Lieutenant) Degiorgio (Sarge said that the LT liked to read mystery novels), and the good Captain Dank's, all report to the '*New Sheriff*' in town', *Don Barnes* (Sheriff and Coroner for all of the Orange County).

Sheriff Barnes was just recently elected to replace the outgoing *Sheriff Sandra Hutchens*. Sheriff Barnes had had a stellar career in Law Enforcement before his present job as the Sheriff for the OC, was well liked by his OCSD deputies and staff.

Charlie liked Sheriff Hutchens, a lot, as he felt that she had done a fantastic job over the past 6-8 years here in Orange County. He thinks that she was formerly a Captain with the LAPD (Los Angeles Police Department).

Charlie is not sure if the good Sheriff Hutchens is a believer in the almighty, or not, however, this he is absolutely sure of she clearly has the attributes of a courageous law enforcement woman, in the way she carried out her duties and responsibilities of Serving and Protecting the honest and law-abiding citizens of Orange County.

Their office is located in Santa Ana, California, very close to the Orange County Criminal Courts building. Sarge investigates complaints about deputies whom make 'errors in judgement' while on-the-job. Like Charlie always says, "There is a bad apple in every bunch." And he also says, "99% of the OCSD are good officers."

Sarge is also involved in assisting the whole of Orange County's good citizens to feel safe and secure with the Law Enforcement Departments and Agencies in Orange County.

Sarge's 'personal' and also the Orange County Sheriff Departments goal is:

1. Integrity without Compromise.

2. Service above Self.

3. Professionalism in the performance of Duty.

4. Vigilance in Safeguarding our Orange County community.

The Orange County Sheriff's Department is certainly not designated as a *Charitable organization*, however, Charlie said that there are lots and lots of great men and women who work for the OCSD and their goals and values listed above are likened to many good characteristics listed in the personal goals of many very famous and quite successful individuals.

The Sarge believed in these among many other good goals and objectives for better Community Policing, so much so that he *risked* his life every day, of every week and of every year for the past 15 years to obtain them.

Sergeant Hernandez told Charlie, in a very worried and yet controlled voice, "There has been *another* shooting in Laguna Woods Village." And he added, that "This is the *third* shooting in the past three weeks."

Charlie absolutely loves LWV (Laguna Woods Village) and has solved crimes there on three separate occasions. He feels that they have the best facilities, the best amenities, as well as the most friendly and wonderful people of any senior retirement community in the country. He really does!

Also, he likes that LWV have about thirty Churches that hold regular services on the sprawling LWV campus. They also have about 250 clubs for anything that you can imagine. They truly do!

In his confidential Private Investigator notes, he referred to those prior criminal investigations in LWV (in conjunction with the OCSD) as: 'A Mystery in Laguna Woods'; 'A Theft in Laguna Woods', and; 'A Kidnapping in Laguna Woods'. Charlie likes to call this his real life 'odyssey,' his Laguna Woods *Trilogy*!

*****

Laguna Woods Village senior retirement community is one of the most prestigious, lovely, friendly as well as safest retirement communities in the United States, and perhaps the whole world. It truly is, Charlie thinks and tells people that all of the time.

LWV just got a new CEO a Mr. Jeffrey Parker. He has a great background in city management and LWV is bigger than a lot of cities in California. He seems like a very capable man with a good vision for the future of Laguna Woods Village.

The former CEO, Thomas Squaritt (age 49) it is rumored, started looking for a new and higher-paying job as soon as he started. He was only here for a little over two years. Great guy with a good sense of humor, but he apparently did not like *old* people. And the Woods is full old people (like Charlie), therefore he decided to move on.

Charlie, as well as Sarge, were both surprised, very surprised, to hear of several recent *shootings* in this beautiful, safe and secure senior retirement community of LWV (Laguna Woods Village). Charlie said to Sarge, "I guess no place is safe from the violence in this crazy mixed up world these days."

The First shooting three weeks ago was when an LWV resident had a *hot* dispute with a building contractor. There are, by the way hundreds of contractors, for every kind of work, crawling all over LWV. Most of them say dumb stuff like, "Laguna Woods Village is like a gold mine." Many of them take advantage of the elderly residents of the Village, however, most are very good and honest workman.

There is so much work to be done here. Most residents, condominiums, and co-ops are fifty-plus years old and are in need of a lot of "TLC" (tender loving care) and lots of it. Plus, new roofs, new plumbing, new sewer lines, and new electrical wiring, to name just a few things but like all older properties, you must keep up with your maintenance on a regular basis, Charlie said.

The dispute that turned violent and ugly as well as ultimately deadly, was over the cost *overrides* of the contractors remodeling of his kitchen. The LWV resident, John Cronin's (a retired lawyer from Boston or New York) had agreed to pay $35,000 for a complete remodeling of his old and quite outdated kitchen.

Charlie does not like attorneys, he really does not. Indeed. And he always says, "Who needs them, they are like a *blight* on our great nation, and the wonderful and very blessed of God, United States of America, they really are."

He personally just had a horrible experience in a very vexating legal matter, with a lawyer whose nickname was the "Lincoln Lawyer" like *Matthew Mc Conaughey* in that great flick and excellent movie by that same name.

Charlie told Sarge, "That attorney, who operates out of his older Lincoln Town-Car works in Santa Ana right by the Orange County court house. His name is Pyke Frederick Meters and he not a very nice person. As a matter of fact, he is a very, very bad man."

The 'Lincoln Lawyer' keeps his confidential legal files in the trunk of his car and sometimes he even sleeps in the back seat when he is broke, according to Charlie.

Don't ask Charlie about attorneys unless you have *several* hours to hear him *bemoan* that particular vocation. Also, if he uses any profanity to describe them, please forgive him.

The Contractor presented him with a bill for $45,000 when it was all said and done. Charlie say it and told Sarge that the kitchen, by the way, looked terrific, it truly did. But he said it should probably have only cost about $25,000 to complete.

Charlie told Sarge, "I will tell you more details of this first, and so sad and deadly Laguna Woods Village incident, soon."

Charlie also told Sarge that he was *keeping* him and his whole big and wonderful family in his thoughts. Charlie was not sure if he was a praying man, either, but he felt by the way Sarge cared about the women, children and the less fortunate people in the OC, it surely appeared that he was a great man.

The second shooting happened just two weeks ago and came about when a retired female LWV board member (Charlie forgot her name), got upset with her next-door neighbor for making too much noise before 8 am and also after 5 pm.

"It had been a long-standing dispute over this seemingly trivial matter," said Charlie. Then he told Sarge, "You are not supposed to do any kind of repair work, or have loud music, and or have *wild* parties before or after those posted times."

The residents of the Woods are absolutely wonderful people however, they are older and do not like to be bothered too early or too late in the day. Charlie, said that he understood completely and that he felt the same way about his neighbors.

And she had shot off a .357 caliber Smith and Wesson revolver (Dirty Harry's = Clint Eastwood's favorite hand gun, what Charlie calls the most 'powerful' hand gun in the world), three times into her neighbor's condominium.

One shot went into the neighbor's master bath room, one into the guest bathroom and the last and fatal shot, into the kitchen. The neighbor who happened to be a very precious 90-year-old lady was washing her dishes by hand.

"That was tragic." Charlie said to Sarge, "Very sad and tragic and completely unnecessary. Things like this should not happen in lovely Laguna Woods nor anywhere else for that matter," he added.

The great OCSD department was short of deputies, several of them had the flu that has been going around lately, therefore, LT. Fred Thompson and his new Captain (Captain Jeffrey Puckett) from the Southwest Division responded themselves.

Even though they both were quite busy with all the paperwork and reports that they have to do on a daily basis, they did not hesitate, even for a second, to jump in their Chevy Tahoe SUV police cruiser and head for Laguna Woods.

And also, one female deputy (Corporal C. Beauhler) was in the neighborhood, and had just wounded the armed suspect in the leg ...instead of taking a *head* shot, and or a *center mass* shot, either one which would have killed the retired board member, immediately.

CHAPTER TWO

NOW, THE THIRD *shooting*, occurred just last week when a wrongfully terminated United Management Services, Inc. employee tried to hold up the ticket booth at the very busy LWV club house number three, or better known as PAC (Performing Arts Center).

They sell lots of tickets for cash as some residents like to save the cost of using a credit card. Also, anyone who robs the PAC would get lots of personal information and paper work from ticket orders and such that vile Identity thieves could use as information to sell to other crooks.

The PAC is located at the corner of Moultan Parkways and Calle Aragon streets in Laguna Woods Village. It has lots of beautiful trees surrounding it and it is a very attractive building. The Board is in the process of remodeling it and updating its quite old and inefficient air conditioning and heating system. Someone on the Board told Charlie that the work was going to cost over Five Million ($5,000,000) dollars.

The PAC has several very good *organizations* that use its many rooms for services on Sundays and also during the week. The

LRF owners of the PAC charge a quite small fee for the use of their facilities at the PAC and also at other locations in LWV.

The great LWV Security Department was called and responded almost at once. Three LWV security guards arrived, and just two minutes later, two OCSD deputies pulled up to assist as 'back-ups.'

The OCSD has patrol units in and out of the LWV on and off every day and year around. They are never far away if the residents need them and are faster than a speeding bullet, as Charlie likes to say.

Charlie told the Sarge that the LWV Security Department was one of the finest of any retirement communities in the whole county. It was headed by Chief *Ray Feldherr*, Security Director.

He used to be a Captain for the great New Jersey State Police and Patrol, a few years back. He has done a remarkable job in revamping the LWV Security department as well as providing better security and a more professional security staff. He had a wonderful wife, Judy. And she used to work for a Security Company years ago.

Then, just as the Sarge and Charlie were exiting close to Club House # 2 and the Ninth Hole Restaurant, at the lovely LWV golf course. It was a *five* (5) Star restaurant, and also a nice cozy coffee shop and a great and well stocked, bar with a quite beautiful view of the golf course and the Saddleback mountains nearby.

The food by the way is just outstanding Charlie said, and the service was just as good. Great food, great drinks, as well as great smiles from the servers. Just, a very pleasant all-around lunching and dining experience. It truly was.

Anyway, they immediately began taking on and receiving *gun* fire. Charlie said It sounded like a rifle with a silencer. He had heard many of them when he was in Iraq and Afghanistan while in the Marine Corp.

Immediately, Charlie said a bunch of *prayers* and hoped for strength and recovery for Sarge as well as himself.

Sarge got hit in the left leg and Charlie got hit in the right arm. Both of the rifle shots were 'through and through' GSWs (gun-shot wounds) and not life threatening, at all ... thank you Dios.

Sarge did not make much of a sound and Charlie just looked at all the blood all over him and 'laughed'. They both had been shot several times before, although I think that Charlie had been hit many more times than Sarge.

Sarge had been in the military as well, an Army Ranger, Charlie said. He also had worked patrol in several OC divisions. He went to the famous OCSD 'Training Academy' and graduated at the top of his class, Charlie said.

Within minutes Sarge and Charlie, were being shot by a 'dirty,' low-down sniper (hidden from view) with a M-30 silenced *Remington* sniper rifle, the OCFA (Orange County Fire Authority) Paramedics arrived within minutes.

And they quickly checked out Sarge and Charlie and told them that they would be alright and then started to take them to the great *Mission Hospital* in Mission Viejo, California.

The Mission Hospital is just south on the 5 Freeway from where they were located in Laguna Woods. Charlie had been there to visit some patients previously and it was a very nice and well-run hospital he thought.

Charlie immediately told the two Paramedics that he wanted them to transport the two of them to *St. Jude Medical Center* in Fullerton instead of Mission and do it as soon as possible.

St. Jude was Charlies Hospital of 'choice', so to speak, since he has been shot and/or stabbed several times. And he had been to several hospitals. Some of them even in Mexico, the Middle East, Europe and the UK (United Kingdom). However, none of them were as good as St. Jude, Charlie told Sarge.

Doctor Anne E. Ford, the best Doctor in the OC (Orange County) and probably the whole state of California, is his personal physician. She is very intelligent, quite knowledgeable of current medicines, and very current on health care procedures, and she is attractive to boot.

Sarge told Charlie, "I think Dr. Ford is the *bomb*, that means hot and smart, just in case you do not know old man? She has a terrific and warm smile, great legs and lovely dark hair. Plus, she is smart and friendly and very caring. I think that I will go to her from now on whenever I get shot and stabbed. What do you think Charlie?"

She is on call, but just for Charlie, 24/7 and she will travel to him if he is too injured to move. Like *today* for example. She once flew all the way to Baghdad, Iraq when he was severely wounded by a hated I.E.D. (Improvised Explosive Device).

*****

The great city of Fullerton is not that far from Laguna Woods therefore Charlie had the Paramedics take the two of them there even though he knew that Dr. Ford would come to them anywhere in the world, if they asked her to.

St Jude (Part of the outstanding *St. Joseph* Medical Group) Hospital is the best in the State, it truly is. They have been around for over 50 years and have a stellar medical record. The Hospital was run by absolutely wonderful Catholic Nuns for many years. And Charlie is not sure if they still run it or if a corporation for profit runs it now.

Charlie and Sarge laughed and told each other jokes as they were being transported to St. Jude. The OCFA *'bus'* (ambulance) had the lights and sirens on so it took no time at all to get to St. Jude in Fullerton.

And the two Paramedics just shook their heads and laughed along with the two injured patients. The four of them sounded like a bunch of drunks at an NFL football game or the crowd at the LWV Clubhouse #3 watching Monday night football games on the big screen with free popcorn and Mexican chips. Charlie and his wife had been to that great and very fun activity a few times.

By the way, Charlie is a big football fan, but his wife is an even bigger one. His favorite team is the *Philadelphia Eagles*, and it just so happens that his lovely wife, Lynn, is from Philly. Of course, they love the LA Rams as the new LA Chargers.

The Chargers are a great football team and they just recently moved here to LA from beautiful San Diego, California. They had been playing ball in San Diego since the 1960's and the whole city bemoaned their moving away, they really did.

St. Jude is just off of the 57 (Orange County) Freeway at the 91 (Riverside) Freeway. Once they arrived at the Hospital, good Doctor Ford was waiting for them in the ER (emergency room). It only took her a few minutes to patch up Sarge and Charlie. She is very good and also very fast.

Afterwards she told Charlie, "Go home and take it easy for a day or two." Charlie then had a big belly laugh and said to Dr.

Ford, "Doc, you know me better than that." Then it was her turn to laugh and she did, a very cute little giggle.

Then she told Charlie, "Charlie call me if you need me, and remember you are not as young as you used to be." Charlie smiled and said, "You know that I will doc."

Charlie and Sarge were back in Laguna Woods or the 'Woods' as Charlie likes to call it, in no time. And our man Charlie was mad, real, real mad. Even though he had been shot several times before, this was the first time he had been *'ambushed'* by a sneaky, despicable sniper, at least as far as he could remember anyway.

Then he and Sarge returned to the site of their ambush as soon as they could hitch a ride from two helpful OCSD deputies stationed in the new Aliso Viejo sub-station.

Charlie found two shell casings, .762 caliber casings to be exact, at the scene of the crime, behind a beautiful big old oak tree. It was located across the street from where they were shot. The Woods Charlie told Sarge had several hundred trees on its pristine and lovely 2,000- acre retirement community.

He also found some footprints size 13 GI boots and a few cigarette butts (Marlboro, remember the 'Marlboro man' commercials back in the day). Charlie told Sarge, "This was the low-life sniper's lair."

Then he asked Sarge, "Who would want to shoot old Charlie? I am a nice guy, right?" Then Sarge replied to Charlie, "Well I am a nice guy as well and who would want to shoot me?" Then they both laughed, again. And Charlie said, "OK, Sarge we are both nice guys and who would want both of us pushing-up daisies, like dead."

Charlie then added, "Sarge we are like the Lone Ranger and Tonto, or Joe Friday and Bill Gannon (remember the great line from Dragnet, "only the facts ma'am only the facts"), the Cisco Kid and Pancho, or Sherlock Holmes and Doctor Watson."

Then he thought for a moment, and then continued, "Yes, or like Spencer and Hawk, or even Bud Abbott and Lou Costello or Starsky and Hutch. Or perhaps, maybe Sonny Crockett *and* Ricardo Tubbs."

Do you recall the outstanding *Miami Vice* T.V. show back in the-day? Charlie used to watch it with his boys every week. Charlie wanted to be a Private Detective ever since he was a little kid. Well, a cowboy first, then a PI.

Sarge then popped up with a big smile on his face and said, "Charlie I want to be Ricardo Tubbs. And you can be Sonny Crockett. What do you think?"

Later on, as they were looking around, Charlie said, "I just had a *'epiphany' I* wonder if it had something to do with one of the cases that I worked on here in the Woods previously?" He had told Sarge before about the fact that he had investigated, and then solved, *three* very high-profile cases here in LWV a few years ago.

He shared with Sarge that the great former OC Sheriff and Coroner, *Sandra Hutchens*, had assisted him in solving those heinous criminal investigations. Charlie said that he really missed her, she was a big asset to the OCSD as well as Law Enforcement in Orange County in general.

The good Sheriff was very smart and she took early retirement to take time to 'smell the roses' and enjoy life a little bit more. She has spent her whole life Serving and Protecting the general public and especially those less fortunate than the rest of us. "Great, great lady, she truly was." Charlie said.

Then Charlie added, "Sheriff *Hutchens* was one of the finest Sheriffs ever in the OC, Orange County, as well as the whole great state of California. She was a wonderful role model for *women* in Law Enforcement everywhere (all over the nation), indeed she was, and still is for that matter.

A little while later Charlie accidentally bumped his recently wounded and shot arm into the car door and he said "Ouch", out loud!" Then Sarge said to him, "Charlie you cry like a baby."

Then he smiled and laughed at his own joke and at Charlie's expense. And Charlie's immediate repose was, "And you whimpered like a little girl when you got shot yesterday." Then they both laughed, real loudly. They were best of friends but they loved to tease each other relentlessly.

Now, back at the old oak tree, Charlie said to Sarge, "I *unintentionally* made some *mortal* enemies when I was here in the Woods before when I solved those *egregious* crimes that I told you about a little while ago."

Charlie said a short little meditation to himself, which he does often throughout the day when he is on a very dangerous criminal investigation, "Thank you gracious Dios for the whole OCSD, the Brea Police Department, Sergeant J.J. Hernandez, Sheriff Barnes, Undersheriff Peterson, the OC District Attorney Spitzer and all of the law enforcement officers and staff in Orange County."

CHAPTER THREE

CHARLIE O'BRIEN *is a Dreamer*, he truly is and he has been a dreamer ever since he was a little kid in rural Ojai (now, Tennis County) California.

He was born in downtown Los Angeles, in what is now called 'Korea Town', then his parents moved Ojai, and after that he grew up in a *barrio* in La Puente and El Monte (San Gabriel Valley), California.

Charlie lived with and went to school with several serious 'gangbangers.' Since they knew him from a kid, they did not stab or shoot him like they did the other *anglo* (white) kids.

He to this very day he loves Latino people, he really does. He told Sarge, "I am part Latino inside did you know?" He thinks Latina women are quite striking with lovely long dark hair and mysterious dark eyes.

Sadly, Charlie did not grow up in a wholesome home. Actually, it was quite dysfunctional, and his father was a drunk, a mean drunk, that is the worst kind. But at least he was a working *alcoholic* and Charlie always had a 'three hot's and a cot,' as convicts say.

Charlie found out not to long before his dad passed away, that he had been a good person when he was young and did not drink much at all back when he was a kid growing up in Iowa. His mother was a wonderful and caring woman but his father, just like Charlie's dad, was an alcoholic as well.

He considers himself a third *Latino* because of being from the 'hood' (neighborhood). He just loves Latin people as well as the wonderful country of Mexico, which he has visited many, many times.

Charlie always tells people that they make the best souvenirs and handmade gifts in Tijuana, Ensenada, and the other border towns. He buys tons of neat hand- made stuff to give as gifts every time he goes there.

When he was small, he wanted to be a 'cowboy' like *Hopalong* Cassidy (Hoppy), or the *Lone Ranger*, the *Cisco Kid*, among many other of his cowboy hero's.

Then as a teenager he fell in love with the noir genre' of police detectives, private eyes, and private investigator. Such as *Mike Hammer*, *Sam Spade*, *Magnum* PI, Harry "*Dirty Harry*" Callahan (e.g. Clint Eastwood).

And also, The A-*Team*, *Columbo*, 77 *Sunset* Strip, *Route* 66, *Horatio* Caine, Miami Vice, *Cannon*, Nick *Carter*, Sherlock *Holmes*, *Kojak*, and the greatest lawyer of all time, *Perry Mason*.

Also, he watched and admired Hercule Poirot, Ellery Queen, Jim Rockford, and Spenser, amongst many, many other great Detective and Mystery TV shows that Charlie watched while he was growing up.

Now days, he dreams that he is Jason Strathan, Liam Neeson, Clint Eastwood, Duane 'The Rock' Johnson, Chris Hemsworth, Kurt Russell, Jackie Chan, or Arnold Schwarzenegger, depending upon the current dream he was having at any particular time.

Charlie the Private Investigator is described as follows: first and foremost, a good and kind man, albeit, he is the first to admit that he is not perfect nor all together, at all.

Charlie is one of the few, true-life *fearless* Detectives in America or so I have been told. He uses his personal and extensive experience which is based upon his solid daily work ethic and personal beliefs, as well as his background of a twenty- year career with the LAPD (the excellent as well as outstanding, Los Angeles Police Department). The LAPD is known and respected all around the world just as the OCSD.

He worked under the great Barnard 'Bernie' *Parks,* one of the *best* police chiefs ever in LA, next to William 'Bill' Parker (whom the city named the Police Headquarters building after), *and* Charles 'Charlie' *Beck,* also one of the most outstanding Chief's LA ever has had, of course.

He was a 'Robbery and Homicide Detective' and he worked on the demonic possessed 'Charlie Manson' family case. As well as many other very high-profile murder cases in LA (Los Angeles). The *madman* and demon *possessed* Charlie Manson, just died recently in prison after being locked up for the past 40 years.

Our man, the good *Charlie* always said that it was too bad that the State of California did away with the death penalty given to Manson (which he fully deserved) for the brutal and senseless killing of several people back in Hollywood in 1969.

Some of the victims were the famous and beautiful actress Sharon Tate (and her precious and unborn baby) who was married to international movie producer, Roman Polanski. Also, there was Jay Sebring, a well know Hollywood hairstylist.

These experiences Combined with his current ten years of being a PI (Private Investigator, or Private Eye as some prefer to call him), gave him the innate ability to investigate and then solve, very large *'White Collar'* crime as well as heinous *'Criminal'* cases in the USA as well as all over the globe.

He finds that by putting his beliefs into action (putting his feet where his mouth is...so to speak) it gives him an edge in understanding, dealing with, and then capturing heinous crooks *and* criminals of all kinds.

Charlie primarily investigates embezzlement cases in the so called *'too big to fail'* banks in the good ole US of A, as well as in foreign countries located all around the world.

He also investigates serious criminal activities as in *'Ponzi' schemes* (think Bernard L. 'Bernie' *Madoff* and his 65 Billion...yes *Billion* dollar rip off of the American public) and also unethical stockbroker/investment bankers (Lehman Brothers, AGI, Manhattan Bank, the Old Merrill Lynch Corporation (now owned and operated by Bank of America).

And one of the 'worst of the worst', *Country Wide Funding* (which was located in the real estate capital of the world, California), the list sadly goes on forever. Charlie wants to find the executives from these evil, and corrupt bank money market fund, and security broker organizations and put them in a *black*-ops prison in Europe.

He also sometimes helps to solve other types of 'criminal' activities that occur in his beloved California, where he hangs his hat (lives). Some of these crimes include bank art theft robberies, kidnappings, crooked *politician's* shenanigans, and bombings, just to name a few.

During Charlie's in-depth investigations as a PI, he frequently encounters some very scary *villains* and heinous and extremely dangerous *criminals*.

He uses his strong and honest beliefs, his devotion to duty, as well as relying on his very sharp mind to assist him in researching and then solving, his very challenging, and complicated, and usually quite dangerous cases.

Charles, albeit, his best friends, fellow Private Investigators (Private Eyes), and LAPD (Los Angeles Police Department) Detectives, and the OCSD (Orange County Sheriff's Department), just call him Charlie. I want you to know that Charlie does *not* enjoy getting older.

As a matter of fact, he hates it... immensely. He truly does. People tell him, “Charlie, you look good for your age.” Kind of a left-handed compliment would not you say?

He realizes that they are just trying to be kind, however, he wishes that instead, they would say to him: “Charlie, you’re still tall, dark, and handsome.”

That would be a big lie but he could whole-heartedly buy into it. He really could. And, besides, he is still tall, and one-out-of-three isn’t bad, right?

He tries and tries, but he just cannot stop good old father-time from marching across his handsome (he wishes) face. In addition, most of his previously nice dark black hair is now turning gray. At least he still has all of his hair, *thank God*!

A lot of his friends are bald and they would kill to have gray hair rather than have no hair at all. Oh, well, we all have our crosses to bear in this crazy old world and his currently is that he just does not have the looks, nor the energy, that he did when he was in his prime.

Charlie now lives in Beverly Hills, California (just west of downtown Los Angeles) which some people call "La-La Land." They are incorrect though, LA is "the City of Angels" ...it is *'Hollywood'* that is really called La-La Land, trust me on that.

He was born and raised here and he most likely will die here...maybe one day soon...you just never know when you will be run over by a big RTD bus or a 400 horse power Dodge Charger (OCSD or a LAPD, police cruiser) chasing a gangbanger in a stolen Mercedes Benz 500S; or even worse, hit by one of the new red-blue-yellow train lines now crisscrossing LA like a scrabble board (or falling dominos).

He actually lives in *Beverly Hills,* California, very close to the majestic and royal blue *Pacific* Ocean. That lovely and one of the most expensive cities in the world to live in and it is located in the United States, is close to the famous city of *Huntington* Beach (*Surf City*, USA).

Remember the *Beach Boys*? Some of them recently performed at the LWV Performing Arts Center. Charlie was told by some residents that it was just an absolutely fabulous concert.

*****

On weekends, Charlie drives his Classic 1964 *Chevy Impala* two-door hardtop. This beautiful ride has been completely restored to the original condition. He just loves classic cars and he has owned several of them over his life time.

He and his lovely wife, like to drive it to *Church* on Sundays sometimes, as well as cruise around in it just for fun. Lots of people give him a 'big smile' when they see him and his wife go by.

His Impala is the Super Sport model with a large big-block 409 cubic inch V-8 HO (high output) *engine*, 4 on the floor stick *transmission* with a deluxe chrome knob shifter. It also has Posi traction non-slip rear end differential and original *Cragar magnesium* wheels from the 1960s.

It has very large and comfortable black leather bucket seats and it is original deep Maroon in color. The engine is all chrome as well as the whole undercarriage.

The whole car is in pristine and mint condition, it truly is. It appraised for around $75,000 recently, however, Charlie would never sell his baby. It is part of his persona and makes him feel young once again whenever he takes it for a spin.

Every time Charlie drives his baby around LA or the OC on weekends all of the old guys and gals and even lots of *Christian* young people at *Church*, give him a thumbs-up. Sometimes they even say, "Old guys with old cars, Rule." Charlie loves to hear that, he really does.

Charlie liked that comment so much that he went out and had several T-shirts made with that saying printed on the back of them. He does not like T's with writing on the front, just on the back for some unknown reason. Some of them are navy blue but most of them are white, naturally.

Also, he has some T-shirts that say, on the back naturally, 'Jesus or Death,' and 'God is not done with me yet, check back with me later', and 'Jesus is Coming, and coming soon.'

The other day as Charlie dressed for work, he *looked* into the mirror. Staring back at him was an extremely handsome angular man, around six feet four with a surfer mop of Pacific Ocean sun-kissed hair.

He had preternatural hazel eyes...so intense that whenever most women looked at him...they had to avert their eyes in embarrassment.

Well, to be just a bit more truthful, at least his eyes *are* hazel, but hardly any women starred at him any longer. He took *another* look, just for fun, and he saw a good-looking man with an angular face topped by a nest of naturally wavy black and white (graying) hair.

And he saw a shy smile, albeit Charlie is anything but shy, but his shy smile made women *swoon*...so boyish and charming, yet masculine at the same time. Charlie you dreamer you!

He had a *six-pack* courtesy of crunches and weight lifting at 24 Hour Fitness and a very strict eating regimen. Then, suddenly he realized that he was just *imagining* what he saw in the little mirror.

So, he decided to take *another* look...a harder look this time and he saw his real self, he thought anyway.

Appearing in his mirror was a very nice looking, *mature* gentleman with a full head of hair, albeit some of it was graying, we'll all right, a lot of it.

He saw friendly-warm yet piercing *hazel* eyes, that sometimes looked blue, other times looked green (Irish eyes are shining) and sometimes even looked brown.

He did not see a six-pack this time around (frown) nor a smile that would make women swoon, sorry Charlie, but you have to know your limitations I am sorry to tell you.

All-in-all, what he saw this time was a man who had lived a very hard life, always worked hard, always, and tried to help others who were less fortunate than himself, and always tried to do his best at whatever tasks laid before him.

Then, he said to himself out loud as usual, "Charlie, you're the man!" Then, he turned and left the bathroom with the image of the *first* man he saw in the mirror, still in his mind's eye.

Do you remember that great old 'Motown' song, "Charlie Brown" by the fabulous *Coasters*? Charlie just absolutely loves Barry Gordy's *Motown* Music, he truly does.

Charlie and his lovely model-looking like wife, Lynn, just saw the fabulous *'Smokey Robinson'* at the Cerritos, quite a marvelous *venue* Charlie says, "Performing Arts Center in southern California."

It was just an unbelievable performance and just to make it even more memorable, Mr. Barry Gordy (yes, *the man* himself) was in the audience. How cool is that? Smokey and Barry live in the same theater. Wow.

Do you remember some of the fun lyrics, "Charlie Brown who walks into the classroom real cool and slow and calls the English teacher Daddy-O. And why's everybody always pickin' on me?"

"Who's always goofing in the hall, guess who? Yeah, you, Charlie Brown." This amongst tons of other great Motown songs, was written by Mike *Stoller* and Jerry *Leiber*, two of the great Rock and Roll songwriters of all time, in Charlie's mind.

Well Charlie has a great sense of humor, he got it from his beloved mama, Vivian Lee. He loves to laugh and he also loves to tell funny stories, and sometimes they are true.

However, some of his fellow Private Detectives, and OCSD, LAPD officers amongst many others, love to sing, "Here comes *Charlie Brown*" whenever they see him after a long period of time.

Some people say that Charlie is a pessimist, but that is just not true. Actually, he used to be a consummate optimist, but he has never been a pessimist, ever.

A glass half-full kind of guy. as they say, however, that was before all of the many 'trials and tribulations' in his life. Also, no, he has said my glass is almost empty.

Now days, he says, “my glass is half-full and half-empty”. That is how the realist looks at things in this crazy, old, mixed- up world that we live in. Life has a way of changing your perspective on one's life over time, does it now?

In addition, our man Charlie likes things simple, real, simple and the simpler the better. He subscribes to that age old saying(adage): KISS (e.g. keep it simple stupid).

Life today is way, way too complicated for him. For one thing, he does not understand computers at all. When he was a kid, they had manual adding machines, and then along came the electric versions.

He used them all of the time and loved them. Even still has some laying around. He also used to be so smart and quick that he did lots of calculations in his head.

He is not exactly sure why, but he cannot do that anymore. Old age, early dementia, perhaps. His cell phone is also somewhat of a mystery to him. It is almost like a tiny, small computer these days.

Someone said to him recently while on an investigation, not a very nice person by the way, that he was *high*-tech challenged. He would have been quite offended, but he was not sure what they meant. So, he just smiled.

Also, he does not know much about the Internet, nor computer software for that matter. Just the other day he heard that he was on the 'dark web' whatever that is?

Bad he knows, but how did he get there and where is it located? In Europe or the far east?

Charlie is going to call *Jan Smoker* and have her explain to him all about the Dark Web and how to get off of it. And also find out who put him on it, and then take care of them. She is a wonderful Christian as well as very intelligent about computers.

And the terms and definitions for computers as well as their software, confuse him greatly. Such as giga-bites, or terra bites, or thumb drives, RAM, different processors, all-in-ones, and on and on for Infinium.

He is planning on taking a computer class from Barbara *and* Craig, at the LWV PC workshop to understand the 'ins and outs' and nuances of the computer world that the old school private eye finds himself living it.

Charlie loves to study his old worn out *Police manual*, every chance he gets. He truly does. Currently he is studying "Illegal Trespassing" in private communities.

The Greek work for 'Blessing' is the word *'eulogia'*, which means to benefit from. Charlie feels that he is blessed above all men with his lovely bride, his lovely home in Laguna Woods Village, and his good friends at the OCSD. These are some benefits that are attached to real life things when he lived them day in, and day out.

CHAPTER FOUR

AS I SAID BEFORE, so sorry but I tend to repeat myself more the older I get, Charlie is a 'dreamer', as I already told you already as well as a dedicated Private Detective and he dreams of a world completely void from all 'evil and heinous' criminals. All types of bad guys and bad gals.

Charlie says that there are lot more bad men in this nutty world than there are bad women, by far, in his personal opinion. Also, and he really hates to admit it, there are tons of bad guys out there too.

Please do not tell any men that he said that or they might get mad at him. He prays for all of the dedicated and loyal men and women in Law Enforcement in the OC every day.

He always tells people that he knows that if that happened, there would be a lot, lot less bad people around. And also, a lot, less bad things happening on this planet, indeed there would.

He meditates for all of the people that he meets in his investigations. Some are from far-away places and do not have a lot of good people to be examples for them.

White collar terrorists, murderers, child molesters, identity thieves, crooked bankers and investment brokers. Drug dealers, pornographers, con-artists and gypsies, dishonest arms dealers, crooked and lying politicians, just to name a few.

Wow, what an absolutely fantastic world that would be, would it not? *See* I told you that he was not a pessimist. He longs for a better, simpler and crime free life style.

Just like Jurassic Park, without all of the big and mean and scary dinosaurs. People would help other people, the rich would help the poor, and people would love one another like family.

Yes, it is quite true that that kind of America *and* world would put him out of a job (being a Private Detective and all), but he could always go back to being a teacher.

Charlie had a very dysfunctional childhood due to an alcoholic and abusive father. Luckily for him, his beloved mama was a real-life saint.

He was born in downtown LA (*Los Angeles*) in what is now Korea-town (Pico and Olympic boulevards) and was raised in a poor and gang 'barrio' in La Puente (close to El Monte), California.

Again, luckily, he grew up with the gang members (some from the infamous *'White Fence'* East LA gang) and they liked him, they said that he made them laugh.

So, they did not stab him with their *'switchblades'* nor shoot him with a *'zip-gun* like they did the other white kids in the neighborhood.

Also, Charlie could speak a little Spanish (pequito) and they appreciated and liked that. He also liked Latino girls and they liked that about him too. He was not prejudiced like a lot of the other white kids.

To this very day, he is still not biased towards others of different nationalities and still loves *Latino* people. They all treated him like one of their own when he had no kind of home life and fed him many times when he was hungry.

Charlie tells people that the only things that helped him survive his rough childhood was his love for *Rock* N' *Roll* music:

Elvis Presley [the King of Rock N' Roll], he learned to sing in his mama's Church.

Carl Perkins [the architect of Rock N' Roll]

Jerry Lee Lewis [the Killer], Charlie and his wife just recently saw him, live.

Chuck Berry [the Fabulous One]

Johnny Cash [the King of Country],

Buddy Holly [the Original One],

Everley Brothers [the Harmony Twins],

Richie Valens [the San Fernando Valley Kid],

amongst many others, way, way too many to list herewith.

And his love for the American *automobile*. Well, alright if you insist, also his love for girls. He had his first girlfriend in the third grade.

She came right up to him on the corner and kissed him on the lips. Wow, he was hooked on the prettier and smarter sex from then on out.

As an adult, Charlie still loves cars, new BMWs but of course Classic cars of his youth, so to speak. When he used to 'cruise' ‘Bob's Big Boy’ drive-in restaurant with car-hops (do you remember those great old days?) in *Pasadena* and also in *Whittier*, California.

Also, the ‘A and W’ *Root Beer* drive-in restaurant in *West Covina*, California (San Gabriel Valley). At both ‘Bob's’ and the ‘A & W’, he would see some of the hottest and fastest cars in southern California. The boys and girls would come from miles away just to 'make the scene'.

Charlie, would look at these fabulous ‘rides’ and drool, and then he would dream of one day having one just like them. He never did get a ‘Hot-Rod’, however, he has had some Fly-cars (hot rides) later on in his life.

Charlie's first car was a used 1949 Chevy (Chevrolet as he likes to call them) Deluxe model four-door sedan. He put a racing cam shaft in it and also put triple-carbs (carburetors) on top of the engine.

He lowered it in front for a Rake look. Some of his Mexican friends were 'low-riders' and they lowered their cars in the back. He put on dual-pipes (exhaust) and moved the stick shift from the steering column to the floor.

It was just a six (cylinder) engine, however, when he was done with it, he could beat other fast Chevys and Fords with big V-8 engines, at the Drag Strips in Irwindale, and or Pomona, California.

*****

Also, he put in white "tuck n' roll" upholstery in the back window and on the seats and new Naugahyde lining on all of the doors. It was light blue in color.

He wanted to buy a newer and faster Chevy two door sedan with a big engine, but just did not have the money since he was a poor kid from the barrio and had to work really hard just to get enough money for his older car.

Charlie has always been, and is still to this day, a Chevy man. He does not know why, he just is. Fords, Chryslers and some foreign cars are alright, but he likes to say, "If you are going to race, go Chevy V – 8 or stay home."

He bought this older but hot set-of-wheels the day he turned 16 years old. When he turned 17, he bought another Chevy (of course), a used 1956 Model 210 two door coupe with a small-block 265 V-8 engine.

It was two-one in color, aqua and white and he dearly loved that ride. It had a three-speed stick on the column and, once again, he moved it to the floor. He always preferred floor shifts for some unknown reason.

He also added dual exhaust, again just as with his last Chevy. He says that if he still had that car today, it would be worth about $35,000. He paid $500 dollars for it back in the day.

Charlie has found out over the years that Classic cars (from the 1950s to the 1970s) are not only fun to 'cruise around' on the weekends, but they are also excellent investments.

For example, a 1957 Chevy Bel-Air two door hardtop coupe, in original mint condition, is worth around $100,000. It only cost about $1,500 or less back when it was new. That's inflation folks.

1953 1/2 Chevy Corvette = $500,000.00

1963 1/2 Ford Mustang convertible = $400,000.00

1970 Ford Mustang 'standard coupe' = Cost new about $5,000.00 and now is worth $25,000.00.

Charlie these days drives nothing but BMW, the "*Ultimate Driving Machine*" with “Efficient Dynamics.” The best made production vehicle in the world, in his opinion anyway. Every day, he thanks his lucky stars for allowing him to own and drive one of the finest cars ever made. Indeed, he does.

A BMW window sticker says, “Intelligently Engineered”. Charlie has one on his BMW. He was looking at a new absolutely beautiful BMW the other day, day dreaming of buying it. The cost $488,000.00 dollars. Wow. That woke him up, fast.

He currently owns two of them. He would have more of them, several different models and such as well as more ‘Classic Cars’, if he had more room in his garage.

He is thinking of building a bigger garage next to his house to make room so that he can buy more cars. As I already told you, Charlie loves cars, old cars, fast cars any kind of car, he truly does.

A new BMW *750* ill Active Hybrid luxury sedan with a 455-*horsepower* engine and that goes zero to 60 in 4.7 seconds, that is fast folks. It is jet black, of course.

Charlie loves fast cars and he always has. Not so much the racing type sports cars, but production vehicles with big and powerful engines. An absolutely beautiful and fabulous ride according to him.

The license plate on this BMW reads 8 BAD 986 (8 Bravo, Alpha, Delta niner, eight, six = in Military code). He wants people to know that he is a Bad dude, at least in his own mind, of course.

And also, A new BMW M-*6* class with a big V - 8 engine and rear wheel drive. Charlie prefers rear wheel drive cars better than front wheel drive. He says that they handle better when you drive them fast.

It has almost neck-*breaking* speed and it does almost 200 miles an hour on the famous <u>Audubon</u> in *Germany*. It has a great 8-speed automatic transmission that you can drive just like a stick shift, if you want to.

It has a hard top that folds neatly up into the trunk of the car. That makes it a cool convertible in the summer time and nice and warm with no rain or wind in the winter.

It also has Black Sapphire Metallic paint, with Aragon custom handmade brown leather seats. Also, it has deluxe 18" BMW alloy wheels, Bluetooth, and a high-tech navigator system.

The license plate number on this BMW reads "I'M PRVT'I" [i.e. as in I am a Private Eye]. He is changing it soon to "I'M PRVIT

D", he thinks that that personalized plate name sounds more like him.

CHAPTER FIVE

SOME PEOPLE SAY that *our* man, Charlie, has the sharp eye of a Falcon, or an *Eagle* (like *Swoop* the Philadelphia Eagle NFL mascot or the toughness of the LA Ram NFL mascot), and a truer aim with a pistol or an automatic rifle that you will ever find.

They always add that old Charlie is a devoted and long -time follower of his personal *Mantra.* That is to say in Charlies own words, "A person should do what they say that they are going to do, but, if they do not do what they promise that they will do, then, they should be held accountable for their wrongful actions".

Also, they say that he was very well thought of by the Police, the CIA, and his fellow private detectives. They go on to add that he never asked them to do anything that he would not do himself, nothing at all.

The people in this very dangerous, line of work, Law Enforcement, et cetera, notice things like that, they truly do. Charlie, they said was always the first man 'through the door' of the bad guy's locations.

And the first person to get shot at or even take a bullet. Most of these former, and present, associates of his always did their best to support him and watch his back whenever they went into battle (got into a gun firefight).

He had been in many quite dangerous, and precarious and life-threatening situations with Howard from the CIA, John from the FBI, the LAPD Police Chief, Charlie (another good guy named, Charlie), amongst many, many other Detectives *and* Private Eyes and even some famed Navy Seals.

All of them down to the very last one, said that Charlie was such a good role model of the 'good guys' that they would always do their utmost for him and even give up their lives for him if necessary.

They said, he was the first to come to the aid of another agent or operative who was in trouble or wounded on a *dangerous* mission. And that he was one of the bravest people that they had ever worked/served with.

All of them, said that they would follow Charlie anywhere, anytime, and any place, and they sounded like they meant it, they really did. He always encouraged the new recruits, new agents, and operatives, always.

Now, if you were to ask Charlie about these 'glowing' and very generous compliments, he will tell you and me that they are not true or that they were overrated.

And that the men and women who made such very gracious comments about him were the real *"hero's"* and not himself. Charlie is actually a modest guy, albeit, you would never guess that by the way he carries himself while on the job.

Also, he would add to that statement, that those kind people were just as brave and courageous as he was, and probably even more so. Well, definitely more so, he would add.

*****

CHARLIE has been shot, as well as stabbed, several times over the years while doing his very dangerous and risky vocation as a Private Investigator. He puts on his body- 'armor' (bullet proof vest), as he goes amongst the *demons* in *this world.'*

That is to say, that by being a LAPD 'Robbery and Homicide' Detective, a covert operative for the CIA and the FBI, the NSA, the OCSD, and working on quite death-defying cases involving some of the most evil and hardened *criminals* in the world he needs and uses God's protection and armor.

And he always adds a true, however very odd sounding comment, he says that he does not mind being wounded nor hurt "on-the-job". That is a little bit of a funny statement don't you think?

In addition, he says that the way he looks at it, getting injured is just an occupational hazard, that's all it is. Very similar to a construction worker losing a finger, or his big toe; or a firefighter (fireman and/or firewoman) getting burned in a raging fire while rescuing men, women, children, and their beloved pets from certain death:

Or, a doctor or nurse who catches a serious (and sometimes even deadly) illness from a very sick patient. Or people that work in factories and foundries who lose arms, legs, and or their lives:

Or a banker who gets shot or stabbed during a bank 'hold-up', or placed and locked in the bank vault without any ventilation. Or any number of other vocations (and there are more than you think) that carry with them the risk of injury or death.

Funny, but the only thing that Charlie ever complains about is not being hurt at the office (kidding). The times in the hospital critical care centers or the long recovery time when he gets home irritates him, that's all.

He hates that the most, he says. And he cannot wait to get back 'on the streets' to investigate and then solve some more heinous *'White Collar'* crimes somewhere in this crazy mixed up world of ours. Just anywhere on the globe is fine with him.

Just like the fearless moderator, John Walsh, of 'America's Most Wanted' real life TV show, it was on Fox Network for years, but now is on CNN. Charlie wants to be out there *'looking for the bad* guys'. Charlie said he believes that John is a *great person.*

John and Charlie both say, "Here in the good *ole US of A*, as well as all over the entire world they will hunt their evil prey." Both of them have traveled thousands of miles around the globe searching for, and locating, evil crooks and criminals. They truly have.

Absolutely nothing in this world makes Charlie happier than when he locates, arrests, and sees them convicted in a Court of Law. It makes him ecstatic it really does.

And then after that, to see them put in captivity in a *dark hole* somewhere. And he always adds, "preferably in a horrible and deplorable '*third* world' prison.

Dios will *mete* out justice of the severest kind imaginable to those who do despicable things to women and children as well as the elderly and the defenseless.

Charlie loves to teach. He used to teach Law *Enforcement* classes at both Cal- State University and Fullerton Community College in Fullerton, California at one time.

He still holds a Life-Time Teaching Credential from the Department of Education in Sacramento, California. And when he semi-retires from being a *Private Eye*, he is planning on going back to teaching at Saddleback Community College in the Orange County or Cal-State University-Fullerton, soon.

Charlie is a big strong and very tough guy, but he is also very gracious and caring at the same time. And he always laughs when he hears someone say, "Here he comes, our man, Charlie Brown," and gives a big old *smile* too.

In real life, Charlie's Lucy is his lovely wife Lynn. Lucy in the cartoon is cute, albeit, his *Philly* girl looks just like a model, she truly does. Also, more importantly, much more importantly, she is an absolutely incredible woman with the *graciousness* and loyalty of the women of olden days.

CHAPTER SIX

CHARLIE, SARGE AND the new Undersheriff *Robert (Bob) Peterson* rolled up to a co-op (similar to a Condo) located at number *666* Calle Aragon in lovely LWV (Laguna Woods Village). The undersheriff joined them at Sarge's request.

The undersheriff works directly under the great Orange County Sheriff and Chief Coroner, *Don Barnes* and also is second in command of the entire OCSD (Orange County Sheriff's Department).

Charlie and Sarge wanted Bob to get a first hand look at the beautiful community that all of a sudden, after 60 years, is having a rash of 'shooting' for some unknown reason.

Bob by the way, Sarge told Charlie, "Bob is very well thought of by all of the rank and file OCSD personnel. Also, he is a career Law Enforcement officer and has been quite successful at every post that he has served on."

Charlie said to Sarge and Bob, "I don't like this address number 666, not one little bit. It gives me the creeps, it really does." Earlier Sarge had got a call from OCSD Dispatch in Santa Ana that someone at this address was brandishing a weapon.

The Dispatch Officer said that he was afraid that there may be another 'shooting' in Laguna Woods Village. And that there had been several lately out there. Right after that earlier call, Charlie, Sarge, and Bob were on the scene in less than 60 seconds.

Even from the outside, the co-op at number 666 looked 'dark and foreboding' to the three investigators. Charlie said to the other two men, "It looks like death to me, for some reason."

Then he added, "Sarge, you and Bob watch your backs." Charlie noticed that it was very quiet, eerily quiet, in other words, way, way too quiet for Charlie's taste.

They started to carefully, very carefully, walk up to the front door. Then Charlie, said to Bob, "Can you cover the rear for us?" And Bob immediately, faster than a speeding bullet, had his 40 Caliber Glock automatic pistol drawn from his custom-made leather shoulder holster (that he bought on one of his shopping trips to Tijuana, Mexico) in his right hand and also a .357 Smith and Wesson revolver in his left hand.

The undersheriff had worked in some very *rough* areas 'back in the day' and he knew how to *get* down when he had too. Sarge pulled out his .45 Caliber auto with a 15 round ammo clip.

Charlie removed his .44 Magnum Smith and Wesson (the Clint Eastwood Dirty Harry gun of choice). Also, he had a Marine K-Bar knife in his belt, in case of any hand to hand combat with whoever was in there.

Just as Charlie and Sarge got to the front door, Charlie heard a little click, which to his keen ear, sounded just like a *shotgun* hammer being pulled back.

Then 30 seconds later, just a heartbeat so to speak, Charlie and Sarge, heard a shotgun blast which went B

bam, bam. That meant that it was a double-barreled shotgun and the perp fired both barrels in very rapid succession.

One second earlier and both of them would have been 'toast,' if you know what I mean. But Charlie had just thrown Sarge into the planter full of soft bushes just to the right of the front door with the madman behind it with his old faithful shotgun.

They landed right under the address on the side of the co-op which when they both looked up showed the spooky address, "666". Charlie felt a shiver go up his spine while he was hiding in the little planter with Sarge.

Some of the shotgun *pellets* hit Charlie in his upper left shoulder and arm and a few hit his big thick neck. Sarge was shot also, he was hit in his left arm and his back.

Thank Abba, neither were wounded very badly, but another trip to the ER at the wonderful St. Jude Medical Center in Fullerton, California with the great and caring Dr. Anne was still in order.

Charlie found out from a local real estate agent, that the co-op at 666 Calle Aragon in Laguna Woods Village is always either vacant and/ or for sale. And it has been that way for the past 55 years.

Charlie said to Sarge, "Not hard to figure that one out old man. That number is bad mojo or bad karma or both, if you know what I mean." Sarge just nodded his head because he knew exactly what Charlie was saying.

Then he replied after a few moments, "Sarge, do you think that the number 666 has some Biblical reference in this case and at this residence?" Charlie responded that the nice and very sharp real estate lady had said to him, "Yes, Charlie perhaps it does, if you believe in that sort of thing?"

Charlie said to the realtor, "Yes, actually I do believe in that sort of thing. I think that is the reason why I am still alive and kicking today, is because of that sort of thing."

After Charlie got up from being shot with the shotgun blast, one blast had hit him and the other blast had hit Sarge, he got mad, real mad, and then he got even madder.

*****

He yelled at Sarge, "I am sick and tired of being shot at for no good reason." Then he kicked open the front door of the co-op which now had a gaping hole right in the middle of it from the two shotgun blasts.

The low down-dirty shotgun-shooter, as it turns out, was a highly bi-polar former Entertainment Director for the property management company LMS, Inc. (Laguna Woods Management Services, Inc.).

He was a tall man, about 6'4" and around 69 years old. And he was a little bit unstable, well a lot unstable, when off of his meds, according to Charlie.

Later on, the shooter said that he thought that Charlie and Sarge were Russian FSB (formerly KGB) agents. Charlie asked Sarge, "Do you think that we look like foreign Russian agents?"

Sarge quickly replied, "I don't think I do, but I think that you do Charlie." And then he had a big belly laugh and added, "Just kidding Charlie, you don't really look like a KGB Ruskey."

Then Sarge laughed even louder, and said, "Alright, no, you don't look like a Russian, but you do look like a very suspicious character." And laughed some more. Charlie said to him, "I am so happy that you have me to make fun of, someone else might be offended by your silly jokes."

Charlie and Sarge love to tease each other even though they are best of friends. Just like Crockett and Tubbs in the hit 1984

Miami Vice TV show. Charlie thinks that he gets the best of Sarge in their battering back and forth.

While Sarge thinks that he comes out on top most of the time. It's probably a 'toss-up' if you ask me. Charlie wins half of the time and Sarge wins the half.

Later, the *undersheriff* put the shotgun kid in the back of his 'black and white' Chevy Tahoe SUV, which had a big block 'police interceptor' 454 c.i. V-8 engine, and swished the shooter off to the OCSD Leo Lacy Jail.

Charlie told Sarge that he was very glad that the Bob had been with them at the shooting also for his help in getting rid of the criminal so quickly. The perp will face some serious time for attempting to kill an OCSD deputy as well as a civilian.

Unless they send him to the mental ward at UCI (University of Irvine Medical Center), of course.

So, Charlie said, "It's sad, but ole number '666' is once again up for sale. The neighbors forced the estate and the relatives of the shooter to sell it. They wanted to get a new neighbor, one who does not wave a shotgun in their faces."

"I wonder," Charlie to Sarge, "Do you know anybody who is interested in buying a haunted house?" Sarge spit back, very quickly, "No Charlie I don't and certainly I would not want to live at that 666 (mark of the *beast*) address."

Then he added, “I would, however, love to live in lovely Laguna Woods Village someday when I get old *like* you Charlie.” Charlie’s response, “Funny Sarge, very, very, funny.”

Later on, Sarge said that it was, “he who shoved Charlie to the ground thus saving his life and not the ‘other’ way around. You know our man Charlie he tends to exaggerate a little bit (or a lot) every now and then.”

CHAPTER SEVEN

CHARLIE KNOWS A GREAT deal about the LAPD (Los Angeles Police Department). He worked for them for many years as a Detective Lieutenant in the 'Robbery *and* Homicide' Division in Hollywood, and since that time, he has worked with them on several very high profile *'White Collar'* crimes in and around the 'City of *Angels'* (Los Angeles), California.

He is not that familiar, however, with the OCSD (*Orange County Sheriff's Department*), therefore he decided to do some background research on the great department since they were the *Lead* Agency in this subject case of the theft of the rare and quite valuable [or even priceless, perhaps] oil paintings by the great masters.

Ray, the excellent and very experienced Chief of the very good *Laguna Woods Security* Department (the Private Security company that monitors and keeps LWV safe), used to be a Commander with the Orange County Sheriff's Department. And, prior to that, he was a State Trooper for 30 years for the New Jersey 'Staties' (New Jersey's Highway Patrol).

Charlie discovered very important background information while doing his normal due diligence and complete research of the OCSD and the private LWV Security Department. He wanted to know all about both of these departments as well as all of the key officers in each one.

Both agencies will be of great assistance to Charlie and his A-Team (all he needs now is Mr. T, remember the great old TV Show the *A-Team* with George Peppard and Mr. T) in solving this vile crime.

And his ever present (omnipresent) spirit of *survival*; shall guide him with this dangerous investigation as well, of course.

Orange County Sheriff's Department History:

The history of Orange County goes back further than the past *100* years and is a tribute to the adventurous spirit, personal drive, and tremendous courage of the early explorers and settlers whose vision and fortitude made cities where there were only dreams.

In any society, there are always challenges, but the pioneer men and women who forged Orange County out of a barren land had the courage to overcome the obstacles that stood in their path.

It wasn't until California became a state in 1850 that formal law enforcement institutions, based on the common law of England, became established. Even then, Southern California was a lawless society until the 1870s, plagued by rustlers, highwaymen, murderers, robbers, and swindlers.

Many made their headquarters in Los Angeles, blatantly defying the law and its traditional keepers-sheriff, jailor, judge and jury. Impromptu, poorly organized vigilante groups supplemented formal law enforcement officials, often taking the law into their own hands, but even these groups were ineffective.

The growth of communities, the increase in the number and proximity of small farms, and the improvement of both education and communication systems finally brought lawlessness under control.

Each formal community had its marshal, its constable, and its judge and when Orange County was formed in 1889, its citizens had a Sheriff directly responsible to them, and a new set of institutions right in their own backyard.

The Orange County Sheriff's Department today is a highly professional organization, which not only continues in its traditional role of crime suppression, but also has expanded into the area of crime prevention.

At the Orange County Sheriff's Department, you can see the spirit of adventure and the same courage as the early settler had. Orange County (as well as Laguna Woods Village) is a place where dreams have become a reality.

*****

The Orange County Sheriff's Department is the law enforcement agency serving Orange County, California. It currently serves the unincorporated areas of Orange County and thirteen contract cities in the county:

Also, Aliso Viejo, Dana Point, Laguna Hills, Laguna Niguel, Laguna Woods, Lake Forest, Mission Viejo, Rancho Santa Margarita, San Clemente, San Juan Capistrano, Stanton, Villa Park, and Yorba Linda, California.

The agency also provides law enforcement services to the Orange County Transportation Authority (OCTA) system and the John Wayne Regional Airport.

OCSD also runs Orange County's Harbor Patrol, which provides law enforcement, marine fire-fighting, search and rescue, and underwater search and recovery services along the county's 42 miles (68 km) of coastline and in the county's three harbors (Dana Point, Newport, and Huntington).

History OCSD:

Early years:

The Orange County Sheriff's Department came into existence on August 1, 1889, when a proclamation of the state legislature separated the southern portion of Los Angeles County and created Orange County.

The entire department consisted of Sheriff Richard Harris and Deputy James Buckley. They had an operating budget of $1,200 a year and a makeshift jail in the rented basement of a store in Santa Ana. They served a sparsely populated county of 13,000 residents scattered throughout isolated townships and settlements.

The problems faced by the first sheriff were typical for a frontier county–tracking down *outlaws*, controlling vagrancy, and attempting to maintain law and order across 782 square miles (2,030 km^2) of farmland and undeveloped territory.

But the county was expanding, and the department grew with it. The Spurgeon Square Jail was opened by Sheriff Joe Nichols in 1897 and the Orange County Courthouse followed in 1901.

Sheriff Theo Lacy (the second and fourth sheriff of Orange County, who served from 1890-1894 and 1899-1911) was able to move from borrowed office space in Santa Ana to a dedicated headquarters in the courthouse that remained in operation until 1924.

When he took office in 1911, Sheriff Charles *Ruddock* commanded a staff of eight full-time deputies and jailers, serving a county of nearly 34,000 citizens.

But the county's frontier past returned to haunt it on December 16, 1912, when Undersheriff Robert Squires became the first member of the department to be killed in the line of duty while he was part of a posse attempting to apprehend a violent fugitive.

The county's growing population brought new challenges. Most of the county had outlawed liquor by the time Sheriff Calvin Jackson took office in 1915. Raids of "blind pig" businesses that served as fronts for illegal liquor sales were commonplace. When Congress passed the 18th Amendment in 1920,

Prohibition became the law of the land. Suppressing illegal liquor operations became a major focus for the department over the next decade. By the time Sheriff Sam Jernigan took office in 1923, rum runners and *bootleggers* were commonplace along the coastline and in Orange County's harbors, using them as a base of operation for smuggling Canadian liquor into the country.

Thanks to Jernigan's diligence, many of them ended up serving time in the new county jail on Sycamore Street in Santa Ana, a building that would serve as OCSD's main jail and headquarters for the next forty-four years. Jernigan remained in office until the end of the decade.

By 1930 the department had grown to include eighteen full-time personnel with an operating budget of $49,582. The county's population was approaching 119,000, over half of which was scattered across a mostly rural landscape.

Sheriff Logan Jackson assumed office in 1931, and for the next eight years guided the department through a turbulent decade. The 'Long Beach' earthquake of 1933 caused widespread damage throughout the county, especially in Santa Ana.

In 1938, a week of intense rain overflowed the Santa Ana River, causing a massive flood that caused over $30 million in damage. The sheriff also had to deal with the Citrus Riots of 1936.

An agricultural labor dispute that led to a strike and subsequent disturbance so large that Sheriff Jackson swore in over four hundred special deputies to help control the violence.

But Jackson's term in office also saw advancements for the department, such as an expansion of the Sycamore Jail that included the county's first radio dispatch center. One of his final acts as sheriff was to implement the wearing of uniforms and a standardized badge for all thirty of his deputies.

Creation of the Reserve Bureau:

Sheriff Jesse Elliott replaced Jackson in 1939, just as the Depression was ending and the county once again began to prosper. This peaceful time was cut short by the outbreak of World

War II in 1941, which created challenges unlike any others in department history.

Most of Orange County's peace officers left for war, leaving the department critically understaffed. This was made worse by the fact that in addition to his normal responsibilities, the sheriff was now required to assist with mandatory civil defense measures, such as air raid drills and blackouts, as well as help police the seven wartime military bases within the county borders.

Elliott suddenly found himself responsible for twice as many duties with only a fraction of his former staff to carry them out. To meet this need, he formed the Sheriff's Emergency Reserve, which eventually became the department's current Reserve Bureau.

CHAPTER EIGHT

CHARLIE OUR PRIVATE Investigator, only one of a few in the nation and the whole wide world, wanted to know a little bit more about the great OCSD (Orange County Sheriff's Department). He feels that knowing more about them, since they are the 'backbone' of Law Enforcement for all of Orange County, California, is crucial to his criminal investigation of a 'shooting in Laguna Woods'.

That way he would be better able to utilize all of their various departments and sections. He also would be able to pray for them as a whole as well as individually, for the good officers that he is working with to solve this heinous shooting case.

Then all of a sudden, Charlie, turned and said to Sarge, "My best amigo, before we look at more Orange County Sheriff's Department (OCSD) history, I just had a little epitaxy and I want to share it with you."

And continued by saying, "They are coming for me, just like they did for 'Porter' and 'Parker' and our Lord and Savior, 'Jesus'. And, I shall meet them on the 'field of Battle', with my loyal and trusted, Sarge."

"And with Abba, out in front of us, we shall go amongst them and defeat our Archenemies at their own game, just like they were nothing."

Then Charlie added, "We shall not fret, we shall not *worry* and we shall not show any *fear* of them nor what they can do to our human bodies!"

"With help from our Dios, we shall *prevail,* we shall be *victorious,* we shall *defeat* them to their last warrior, and then we shall be *vindicated.*"

After that, Charlie tacked on, "Sarge, you need to read and memorize more thoughts and ideas from the Book I told you about, remember?"

Now, it was Charlie's turn and he said, "Sarge lets back to the research on the history of the OCSD."

<u>Post-World War II:</u>

In 1946, retired **NFL** star and former deputy ***James A. Musick*** came home from the war and successfully ran for the office of sheriff, assuming command in 1947. He would serve as sheriff for the next twenty-eight years–the longest term in department history.

When he took office, the county was still mostly rural, with a population of 216,000 served by a department of only seventy-six. During Musick's administration, a number of divisions and facilities were commissioned that remain active to this day.

He implemented the county's first crime lab, its first Peace Officer's Training Center (now known as the Katella Facility), and the nation's first law enforcement Explorer post.

The 1960s saw the construction of the Orange County Industrial Farm (later renamed the James A. Musick Jail Facility), the Theo Lacy Facility, and the headquarters and central jails still in use today.

In response to the civil unrest of the late 1960s, Musick formed the Emergency Action Group Law Enforcement (EAGLE) team, a group of deputies with specialized training in various riot control and specialized tactics.

Although the team disbanded several years later, certain platoons evolved into the modern-day SWAT, Hazardous Devices, and Mounted Patrol units. The department grew even larger when the Coroner's Office merged with it in 1971.

By the time Musick retired in 1974, the county had expanded to a rapidly urbanizing population of over 1,400,000, with the department having grown to a staff of over 900.

Musick's handpicked successor was *Brad Gates*, who became sheriff in 1975. The department continued its rapid expansion during his administration, with the merging of two more agencies, the Orange County Harbor Patrol and the Stanton Police Department.

In response to severe jail overcrowding, the Intake Release Center was opened in 1988, completing the modern-day Central Jails Complex.

Gates also established the Air Support Bureau and created the Laser Village tactical training center, as well as the county's first DNA laboratory. The continuing urbanization of the county resulted in several cities incorporating and becoming contract patrol areas.

Gates also steered the department through the challenges of a severe county bankruptcy in 1994. By the time he retired in 1999, the department had grown to over 3,000 members.

Sheriff Carona:

Sheriff ***Michael Carona*** took office in 1999 and oversaw a merger of the Orange County Marshal's Department (his former agency) with OCSD. His term brought additional department expansion, including a modernized Katella Facility and a new OCSD Academy in Tustin.

Patrol cars were equipped with mobile computers, and anti-terrorism units were formed in response to the events of September 11, 2001. Carona received an initial surge in popularity due to the department's handling of high-profile cases such as the Samantha Runnion abduction and murder.

In 2007, Carona and a few of the former members of his executive staff were replaced. The county wanted some new blood, so to speak, in the quite large and complicated to manage, OCSD.

Carona's replacement, retired L.A. Sheriff's Commander *Sandra Hutchens*, was appointed by the county Board of Supervisors after a nationwide search for a suitable candidate.

Hutchens reorganized the agency after assuming office and created new branches such as the Homeland Security Division, a unified command for the various bureaus responsible for the county's security.

Subsequent economic challenges required large cuts to the department's budget and made it necessary to streamline the entire agency. Like a lot of big organizations Channel Design (Downsizing and/or *Mitigating*) is quite difficult to do, however, Sheriff Hutchens *and* her Executive Staff did a superb job.

*****

Beds for Feds:

In 2010 OCSD and **Immigration and Customs Enforcement (ICE)** reached an agreement that would allow federal detainees to be placed in Orange County Jail facilities. Several deputies have been cross trained as ICE Special Agents.

Organization:

The OCSD is divided into twenty divisions covering five organizational functions: Public Protection; Jail Operations; Technical Services such as investigations, coroner services, emergency management; and Administrative and Support Services.

The Orange County Marshal's Department was absorbed by OCSD on July 1, 2000, then-Sheriff **Michael Carona** was the last Marshal. OCSD, under its Court Operations Division, now provides all security and law enforcement services (such as Bailiff services, weapons screening checkpoints, and prisoner custody) to the county court system.

The OCSD currently has 1,460 sworn deputies and over 1,446 civilian personnel, with another 800 reserve personnel.

Command Staff:

Executive Command:

Sheriff-Coroner, Undersheriff, Community Services, OC Crime Lab, and Public Affairs.

Administrative Services Command:

Executive Director and Senior Director

Communications and Technology

Financial/Administrative Services

Research and Development

Support Services

Custody Operations Command:

Assistant Sheriff, Commander, Central Jail Complex, Musick Facility, Theo Lacy Facility, and Inmate Services

Professional Services Command:

Assistant Sheriff, Commander, Court Services Bureau, Professional Standards, S.A.F.E., and Training Force

Field Operations and Investigative Services Command:

Assistant Sheriff, Commander, Coroner Medico Legal Investigations, and Airport Operations

Homeland Security, Investigations, North Operations, South Operations, Stanton Police Services, San Clemente Police Services, and OCTA Police Services

Charlie needed to take a break from his investigation into the OCSD. He had to make an encrypted cell Phone call to the FBI office in LA.

CHAPTER NINE

CHARLIE, OUR VERY famous or infamous some people would say, Christian Detective now continues his information gathering into the excellent OCSD (*Orange County Sheriff's Department*). He found a lot of info on the great 'Agency' and he felt that it may come in handy with his investigation into his *'Shooting in Laguna Woods'* criminal investigation and case later on.

He listed and emailed this important additional background (besides the information that he had already sent previously) to Jan Smoker, his outstanding cohort with his criminal investigations for the past five years, and also to the FBI, CIA, and also himself (to save on his office computer hard-drive, for future reference).

Sworn:

Sheriff-Coroner (1)

Undersheriff (1)

Assistant Sheriff (4)

Commander (3)

Captain (12) / Chief Deputy Coroner

Lieutenant / Assistant Chief Deputy Coroner

Sergeant / Supervising Deputy Coroner

Investigator

Deputy Sheriff II / Senior Deputy Coroner

Deputy Sheriff I / Deputy Coroner

Reserve Deputy Sheriff

Non-sworn:

Sheriff's Special Officer III

Sheriff's Special Officer II

Sheriff's Special Officer I

Sheriff's Crime Scene Investigators

Sheriff's Correctional Services Assistant

Sheriff's Community Services Officer

Sheriff's Correctional Services Technician

Sheriff's Crime Prevention Specialists

Sheriff's Professional Staff

Sheriff's Cadets

Sheriff's Explorers: Explorer Commander (1):

Explorer Captain (4)

Explorer Lieutenant

Explorer Sergeant

Explorer Corporal

Explorer

Probationary Explorer

Facilities and Equipment:

Field and Investigative Services Command.

Homeland Security Division:

The division is composed of five separate bureaus, each with a nexus to local homeland security. Each one is run by a lieutenant or administrative manager. These bureaus are led by a Captain.

Special Enforcement Bureau (SWAT section/Air-Support Unit/Hazardous Devices Unit/Tactical Arrest Team/Crisis Negotiators Team).

Mass Transit Bureau (OCTA /Explosive Detection Unit/Module-Rail section).

Marine Operations Bureau (Newport Beach Station/Dana Point Station/Sunset-Huntington Station).

Mutual-Aid Bureau (Counter Terrorism section-JTTF/Grants/ Sheriff's Response Team).

Orange County Intelligence and Assessment Center.

North Operations:

North Operations includes patrol and investigative services for the northern boundaries of Orange County. This division is based out of Sheriff's Headquarters in Santa Ana, California.

Villa Park, California

Rossmoor, California

Midway City, California

Orange Park Acres, California

Silverado Canyon, California

Modjeska Canyon, California

Yorba Linda, California

Unincorporated Anaheim, California

Unincorporated North Orange County

Emerald Bay, California

Stanton Police Services:

Stanton Police Services includes patrol and investigative services for the city of Stanton, California after the Stanton Police Department was absorbed by OCSD. The current head of Stanton Police Services is a Lieutenant.

Stanton, California

*****

South Operations:

South Operations includes patrol and investigative services for the southern boundaries of Orange County. In 2015, South Operations was bifurcated into Southeast Operations and Southwest Operations. Southwest Operations is based in Aliso Viejo and led by a Captain.

Southwest Ops consists of the city's south and west of the I-5 freeway, Aliso Viejo, Laguna Hills, Laguna Woods, Laguna Niguel, San Juan Capistrano, Dana Point, and San Clemente.

Southeast Operations is based in Lake Forest and led by a Captain. Southeast Ops consists of the city's north and east off of the I-5 (Santa Ana) freeway.

Lake Forest, Mission Viejo, and Rancho Santa Margarita. Southeast Ops also houses the South Patrol Bureau, led by a Lieutenant. South Patrol Bureau provides general law enforcement services to the unincorporated communities of Wagon Wheel, Coto De Caza, Dove Canyon, Trabuco Canyon, Las Flores, Ladera Ranch, and Rancho Mission Viejo.

Aliso Viejo, California

Dana Point, California

Laguna Hills, California

Laguna Niguel, California

Laguna Woods, California

Lake Forest, California

Mission Viejo, California

Rancho Santa Margarita, California

San Juan Capistrano, California

Coto de Caza, California

Las Flores, California

Ladera Ranch, California

Wagon Wheel, California

Trabuco Canyon, California

Ortega Highway, California

San Clemente Police Services:

San Clemente Police Services includes patrol and investigations for the city of San Clemente, California. In 1992 San Clemente Police Department was absorbed into OCSD, however San Clemente only allows the former San Clemente Police Station to be used by deputies who patrol their city. The current head of San Clemente Police Services is a Lieutenant.

San Clemente, California

Orange County Harbor Patrol - Marine Operations:

Orange County Harbor Patrol includes maritime security and enforcement of laws in Orange County's Harbors. Sheriff's personnel frequently work in conjunction with Federal Homeland Security and United States Coast Guard for interdiction of contraband and human trafficking. The current head of Harbor Patrol is Orange County Harbormaster, a Lieutenant.

Sunset Beach Harbor, California

Newport Harbor, California

Dana Point Harbor, California

John Wayne Airport Police Services:

John Wayne Airport Police Services provides responsive and professional service to John Wayne Airport. The Bureau consists of Deputy Sheriffs and Sheriff's Special Officers along with Explosive Detection Teams.

They pro-actively protect lives and property at this facility and respond to all calls for service promptly. In addition to these services they remain vigilant against threats (foreign or domestic) to ensure the security and safe operation of this facility.

All Airport Police Services employees are expected to represent the department and John Wayne Airport in a friendly, helpful, and professional manner. The current head of John Wayne Airport Police Services is a Captain.

John Wayne Airport:

OC Transit Police Services:

The mission of the OCTA Transit Police Services is to maintain a safe and peaceful environment for OCTA customers and employees, and to ensure the security of OCTA property. The current head of OCTA Police Services is a Lieutenant.

Orange County Transit Authority:

Training Division:

The Training Division develops, schedules, and presents law enforcement training for sworn peace officers and professional staff. The department utilizes two training sites ensuring the best learning environment possible, depending on the specific needs of the course.

Advanced officer training is primarily conducted at the Katella Facility in Orange. Academy and entry level training is primarily conducted at the Sheriff's Regional Training Academy in Tustin.

The Orange County Sheriff's Department, as well as multiple local, state, and even federal public safety agencies, train at and utilize both sites.

Extensive input from law enforcement and other leaders throughout the county help to mold the curriculum and training that is offered. Both facilities are often utilized seven days per week and include daytime and evening instruction. The Division is led by a Captain.

The Orange County Sheriff's Regional Training Academy is located in Tustin, California on the site of the former Tustin Marine Corps Air Station. The facility opened in late 2007 and replaced the old academy on Salinas Avenue in Garden Grove which was no longer adequate due to overcrowding.

The Orange County Sheriff's Regional Training Academy produces highly trained and professional Deputy Sheriffs & Police Officers, Sheriff's Special Officers, and Correctional Services Assistants. Some training is also conducted at a Sheriff's facility on Katella Avenue in the city of Orange, California.

The Katella Training Facility in Orange, California houses the qualifications range, tactical range, administrative offices, advanced officer training, and elements of Homeland Security Division's Special Enforcement Bureau.

Some of the Orange County municipal agencies that send their recruit officers to OCSA include Newport Beach Police Department, Laguna Beach Police Department, Irvine Police Department, Costa Mesa Police Department, and University of California Irvine Police Department.

And also, the Fullerton Police Department, Garden Grove Police Department, Westminster Police Department, La Habra Police Department, Brea Police Department, Placentia Police Department, Tustin Police Department, and Orange Police Department.

Orange County residents are not the only recipients of the Orange County Sheriff's Academy's highly trained peace officers. Many Los Angeles County municipal police agencies send their recruits to be trained by the best at OCSA. Some of these agencies include;

Beverly Hills Police Department, Santa Monica Police Department, University of California Los Angeles Police Department, Torrance Police Department, Hawthorne Police Department, and Palos Verdes Estates Police Department.

And also, the Redondo Beach Police Department, Manhattan Beach Police Department, South Gate Police Department, Burbank Police Department, and Glendale Police Department.

CHAPTER TEN

THE LAST OF the quite important background about the OCSD that Charlie passed on to his 'A-Team' assisting him with the 'Shooting in Laguna Woods' criminal case is listed herewith:

> *The Sarge has spent ten years with the great Orange County Sheriff Department and he added some facts about the great law enforcement organization to Charlie. Charlie knew more about the LAPD (Los Angeles Police Department but Sarge knew more about the OCSD.*
>
> *They often shared stories about each- others favorite agency. While Charlie dearly loved the OCSD his hear was still with the LAPD where he worked for 20 years. Here is what Sarge added to what he had already shared with Charlie about the OCSD.*

Jails:

OC Central Jail Complex in Santa Ana, California.

The OCSD Custody Operations Division operates four (4) jails:

Central Men's Jail and Women's Jail - The Central Jail Complex, opened in 1968, is located next to the department offices in

Santa Ana. It houses approximately 2,664 inmates. In January 2016, three inmates escaped from the jail.

Intake Release Center (IRC) - In 1988, as a part of the Central Jail Complex, the Intake Release Center was built to facilitate the intake and processing of inmates, and the including medical screening, booking, proper identification, and transfers between facilities.

While it is a transitional facility, it also holds male and female inmates for brief periods.

Theo Lacy Facility - The TLF, located in the city of Orange, was originally built in 1960. A major expansion, completed in 2006, brought its capacity to 3,100 inmates, making it the largest jail in the county.

James A. Musick Facility - A minimum security facility located on unincorporated county land near Lake Forest and Irvine, "The Farm" provides custodial and rehabilitative programs for 1,256 adult male and female inmates.

Courts:

After the Orange County Marshal's Department was absorbed by OCSD, the Sheriff's department became responsible for providing court services. There are Sheriff's personnel stationed at the Justice Centers throughout the County.

Sheriff's staff at the Justice Centers fulfill the vital mission of the Sheriff that include bailiff services in each courtroom and weapons screening operations in the lobby of each Justice Center. Each justice center houses a detention holding facility for inmates who are appearing in court each day.

These detention facilities are staffed by Deputy Sheriffs. There are also Deputies assigned to Civil Bureau who are out every day serving court documents, serving restraining orders, and conducting evictions.

The Special Operations and Judicial Protection Unit provides specialized protective and investigative services to counter any threats, perceived or real, towards the judiciary of the Superior Court of California, County of Orange.

All of these personnel fall under the Court Operations Command of the OCSD Professional Services Command. The current head of court operations is Captain Jim Rudy.

Orange County Sheriff's Offices are located at the following Superior Court of California facilities in the County of Orange:

Central Justice Center (CJC) in Santa Ana, CA

Lamoreaux Family & Juvenile Law Justice Center (LJC) in Orange, CA

North Justice Center (NJC) in Fullerton, CA

West Justice Center (WJC) in Westminster, CA

Harbor Justice Center (HJC) in Newport Beach, CA

Aircraft:

The department's 5 helicopters are (3 Euro copter AS350 B2 (or "A*Stars") and 2 rescue UH-1H Huey's) that use the radio call sign "Duke" (after actor and former Newport Beach resident John Wayne) and, appropriately, use John Wayne Airport as their operational base.

The original "Duke" helicopters (a pair of Boeing 500's) had an image of John Wayne riding atop a sheriff's badge (while waving his cowboy hat) painted on the fuselage.

The Aviation Unit covers the 13 contract cities the department serves, unincorporated communities, as well as a contract with the Santa Ana police department.

*****

Orange County Sheriff's Department Explorer Post 449:

In November 1959, Orange County Sheriff James A. Musick wanted "young men," who desired exposure in the field of law enforcement to be afforded the opportunity to do so.

In a newspaper article he stated, "We organized the group after we found that other special interest Explorer Posts were taking our best young men from our high schools.

We decided, rather than take what was left over after other fields of endeavor took the best, that we should start training young men of high school age now for a career in law enforcement."

Thus, the first Law Enforcement Exploring Post in the nation was established. Its purposes were, "To train young men of today for the future that awaits them in the law enforcement field of tomorrow.

To stimulate young men's interest in law enforcement practices, the code of ethics, and the fine qualities of citizenship which are expected, to briefly explore all phases of law enforcement, and to be a definite approach to juvenile decency."

Post 449 began with twenty-eight explorers in Santa Ana who had to meet the qualifications of being between 14 and 21, must maintain a "B" average in school, have a clean record, be of outstanding citizenship in their community, and have a general reputation beyond reproach."

In 1973, after fifteen years of only young men being allowed in the Exploring program, Boy Scouts of America allowed young women to explore careers in law enforcement through membership in an Explorer Program. Maintaining the same high standards for qualification and training these young women diversified the Department's Post.

When the residents of contract cities and the unincorporated county area need help, they call the Sheriff's Department; when the Sheriff's Department needs help, they call on their Explorers.

The 'Orange County Sheriff's Explorer Post' supports deputies during road closures caused by natural disasters such as mud-slides, floods, and forest fires. They complete search missions where either missing persons or evidence is sought and are deployed to protect crime scene perimeters.

This involvement by the explorers allows Deputies to be available for calls for service. Explorers are also used to assist in public education. They distribute brochures explaining changes in parking regulations or temporary street closures.

During Bicycle Rodeo Events, Explorers demonstrate to children how to properly size and wear bicycle helmets. They offer child identification and crime awareness, through a "Kid-Print" program and assist in crime prevention demonstrations throughout the county.

The Department's Explorers serve the community by providing crowd and traffic control during Basic Academy Graduations, County Building Dedications, Mall grand openings, Community awareness fairs, 10 K runs, parades, and a multitude of other charitable events.

The Post's Color guard is used to present the flag at City Council and County Board of Supervisor meetings, as well as scouting and civic events.

The Orange County Sheriff's Department 'Explorers' participate in Law Enforcement competitions throughout the state. Through the use of the Department's "Laser Village" and its Training Staff, Post 449 Explorers have learned skills which enabled them to win several awards in Felony Car Stop. D.U.I., Bomb Threat and Search and Building Search scenarios. The Explorers also compete in Tug-of War, Volleyball and Obstacle Course competitions.

Sheriff's personnel, who volunteer as Advisors for the Department's Post, contribute countless hours exposing youths to Law Enforcement Careers. Their commitment to the advancement of the Exploring program goes beyond the Department's Post.

The Department's advisors also serve on the County-wide Organization as Ranking Officials, Academy Directors, Tactical Training Officers and Instructors at the Explorer Academy.

In addition to Orange County, these Advisors have trained and taught Explorers in Kern, Los Angeles, San Diego, Riverside, and Ventura counties.

List of the excellent, very devoted and outstanding former sheriffs:

Richard T. Harris (1889–1891)

Theo Lacy (1891–1895)

Joe C. Nichols (1895–1899)

Theo Lacy (1899–1911 = second term)

Charles Ruddock (1911–1915)

Calvin E. Jackson (1915–1923)

Sam Jernigan (1923–1931)

Logan Jackson (1931–1939)

Jesse L. Elliott (1939–1947)

James A. Musick (1947–1975)

Brad Gates (1975–1999)

Michael Carona (1999–2008)

Jack Anderson (Assistant Acting Sheriff)

(January 2008 to June 2008)

Sandra Hutchens (2008–2018)

Don Barnes (2018 - present).

CHARLIE FELT LIKE he now knew a tremendous amount more about the great OCSD and their excellent current Sheriff (Don Barnes). After all of the above research and talking to lots of people inside, as well as outside, of the department he is very comfortable with letting them be the *Lead* Investigative Team in the *"Shooting in Laguna Woods" Village*.

The local Sheriff's Department Patrol site is located in Aliso Viejo, California, which is very close to the Laguna Woods Village. Their excellent Officer's patrol LWV 24/7, and *Charlie* noted their patrol cars several times while on the job at LWV.

Normally the *FBI* takes over control on a quite high-profile case such as this one because they want the National exposure (i.e. press and news coverage), however, *Charlie* insisted that the *OCSD* could handle it with the assistance of the FBI and himself, of course.

CHAPTER ELEVEN

CHARLIE CALLED HIS favorite C.I. (confidential informant) Jan Smoker recently retired from her executive assistant Director post at the CIA (Central Intelligence Agency). She was also the Director of International Operations in the dangerous Middle East. Also, she still had great connections at the 'Agency' even though she was now retired.

Charlie told Sarge when Sarge asked him, "Charlie old man, I do not know much about the CIA, but I do know a lot about the OCSD, of course, and also the FBI (Federal Bureau of Investigation)..." Charlie instinctively interrupted him and said "You mean the Federal Bureau of *Intimidation*?"

Sarge laughed, loudly and said, "Right you are Charlie, they Intimidate more than they Investigate, sometimes, but I know of lot of their southern California Agents, and they are all good people."

And, then Sarge added, "I think I may want to work for them (FBI) someday, what do you think Big Busy?" Charlie pondered for a few seconds, and replied, "Sarge I think you would make an excellent FBI Agent I really do."

Charlie added, "You are quick, think good on your feet, and seasoned on the *mean* streets of 'Santa Ana, California' and Street Smart but you cannot shoot a fish in a barrel, ha, ha." Charlie, I think he fine's it hard to give compliments to his loyal partner and side-kick, but he thinks the world of him, and would give 'his life' for him if he needed too, he truly would.

Then, Charlie said to Sarge," Listen my niño (son), and I shall enlighten you on the CIA, just a summary of course, we do not have all day you know? Charlie stated out by saying, "First of all they liked to be called The Agency" and not the CIA." The CIA has a bad reputation, somewhat deserved but not completely, to a lot of people especially in a lot of foreign countries.

Then Charlie, told Sarge the following information on the CIA. Charlie knows all about the 'Agency' as he has worked with them on criminal cases in foreign countries for the past twenty years.

He said, "The Central Intelligence Agency was started on September 18, 1947 very soon after the end of World War II. It has about 21,000 employees and their 'unofficial' motto is "You shall know the truth and the truth shall set you free." (Taken from John 8:32 in the Bible).

The Agencies annual budget, which comes from taxpayers like you and I, is about 15 Billion dollars (yes, I said Billions and not just Millions). Charlie told Sarge that a lot of the money that the

CIA spends is wasted because the Dictators *and* Despots in a lot of foreign countries steal most of the money and do not give it to their people nor use it for what the *Agency* gave it to them for.

Now back to the case, Charlie wanted to know what, if anything she had found out about the list of names of the suspects that he had given her recently. Her contacts should have turned up some good intel (Intelligence) about them by now.

Charlie told Sarge, "If there is any 'dirt' on these low life's, any at all, Jan and her contacts will find it, and they will not stop until they find something. Everybody has something in their pasts to be ashamed of, everyone."

Charlie said to Sarge, "If you have a few minutes, *amigo*, I want to tell you about the other three (3) criminal investigations which I was involved in during recent years here in lovely Laguna Woods Village.

The first investigation, let's call it case number one, is described in my confidential investigation notes located on my hard-drive computer in my Private Investigator office."

Case number one:

"A Mystery in Laguna Woods" takes place in Laguna Woods, California one of the most beautiful, friendly, as well as safest

senior retirement communities in the whole United states and most probably anywhere on the globe.

Our man Charlie was hired by LMS, Inc. (Laguna Management Services, Inc.) to investigate the brazen theft of seven (7) priceless and original oil on cavass paintings by some of the greatest painters of all time.

LMS, Inc., is the property manager for the owner of all 2,000 acres of Laguna Woods Village. LMS, Inc. has one of the best CFOs (Betty) of any HOA management company in the country, bar none, according to Charlie.

The actual real estate owner of Laguna Woods Village, is PRF (Preferred Rainbow Foundation) and they are worth over One Billion dollars. And they have some top-notch and quite bright volunteer board members, a few of which are: Ms. Diane Phelps, Treasurer; Mrs. Joan Milliman, Secretary; and Mrs. Annette Sabol Soule, First Vice President, among several other board members.

These exquisite 'old masters' Works of Art had been on display at the LMS, Inc. resident Community Center located at 24351 El Toro Road, Laguna Woods, California, in lovely Laguna Woods. All of the visitors as well as all of the residents just loved looking at, and admiring, them whenever they came to the Center.

The quite famous "Christie's" *auction* house in London, England (the UK) had valued them at One Billion dollars. They were insured by Lloyds of London Insurance Carriers for one half-billion.

That meant that LMS (and in actuality, the residents) would not have to come up with half-million to replace the gorgeous Master Pieces.

Charlie solved that case with the keen assistance of his A-Team. His team was in part comprised of: Howard Stewart ex-CIA Director, *Jan Smoker*, and the great men and women deputies of the *OCSD*.

The art theft mastermind, and career criminal, turned out to be a very tough Serbian woman named *"Olivera Vasic Cirkovic"* and what a piece of work she was. Along with her three members of her *'Blue Canaries'* world -wide art theft gang of thieves and thugs.

The 'Blue Canaries' got their idea of how to operate and avoid capture from the quite famous *'Pink Panthers'* theft gang that terrorized high end jewelry stores, diamond brokers, and even banks back in the 1980's and 1990's.

Charlie told Sarge, "Some day when you have some extra time, look up *'Pink* Panthers' on the internet and you will be amazed at what all they did and how many places they robbed during their long 'crime' spree."

Case number two:

"A Theft in Laguna Woods" also took place in lovely Laguna Woods, which is only about ten minutes away from one to the most beautiful and romantic cities in the whole wide world, Laguna Beach, California.

Once again, Hefa Charlie was contracted by LMS, Inc. (Laguna Management Services, Inc.) to investigate the heinous and vile 'Cat' *burglaries* in one of the safest and well protected retirement communities in the nation.

Charlie well knows that for law enforcement officers, there is no such thing as a *routine* 'traffic stop', not at all. You can be run over on purpose and/or by accident, stabbed, sapped, assaulted, and at the very least cussed- out and spit upon.

A very astute and on the ball OCSD deputy was patrolling a section of the Santa Ana Freeway (the 5) going south toward San Diego and Tijuana, Mexico. A SUV was doing about 100 miles per hour and he decided to pull over the jet-black Cadillac Escalade over for speeding.

It had paper places on it (so it could not be identified and it had been stolen just two days ago from a car dealership in Laguna Hills. And all of the widows were tinted with that limo-reflective window tinning. Which meant the deputy could not see anything inside of the SUV.

This is a very, very dangerous situation as Charlie well knows being an ex-LAPD officer for twenty years on the mean streets of LA (Los Angeles). The OCSD deputy immediately called for backup from the Aliso Viejo southwest sub-station where Captain Jeffrey Puckett was in command.

In less than a heartbeat, it seemed like, three OCSD units rolled up on the precarious scene. One deputy was a woman officer named C. Beauchler a thirty- year veteran of the OCSD and knows the Laguna Woods area like the back of her hand.

Deputy Beauchler asked the stopping deputy (name?) to cover her as she approached the very suspicious looking black Caddy. She pulled out her trusty pistol with her right hand and then reached down and took out the emergency .38 revolver on her left ankle.

With both guns drawn and aimed directly at the black SUV, she carefully, very carefully approached the driver's side window. She tapped hardly on the still closed highly tinted window, and it slowly, very slowly came down, but only about six inches. Inside were five people, one woman and four men. And they all looked very suspicious to her.

*****

She said to the driver, "Let me see your hands. NOW." He put his hands on the steering wheel and smiled at her, he had big shiny teeth. He was not afraid in the least she could tell that right away.

At the same time one of the other deputies from the southwest division, was standing at the passenger side door window with a shotgun pointed at the head of the passenger and she was moving it back and forth from the passenger to the back seat where three more people were seated.

One was a woman and two were males. They all looked deadly, very, and smelled like crooks. Cops and Sheriffs can smell a perp (perpetrator) from a mile away. Deputy Beauchler told all five of them to get up on the vehicle, get down on their knees and put their hands -on top on their heads.

Surprising to all of the four OCSD deputies, the five suspects all complied immediately and also now they were all smiling, for some unknown reason. Later she was to find out that they had been arrested all over the world before and they always made 'bail' and got out of that country before the Trials.

The other deputy with the shotgun covered them like a 'blanket' while deputy Beauchler hand cuffed them and then told them to lie face down on the side of the 5 freeway. It was about a quarter after one (1:15 am) when they made the 'routine' stop.

Then deputy Beauchler opened the back of the SUV and found five police scanners, 5 automatic rifles, 10 semi-automatic pistols, and very surprisingly she also found 30 women's purses, and20 men's wallets.

She noted right away that all of them were from men and women who lived in Laguna Woods Village senior retirement center. She knew that area quite well as she patrolled it every day to keep the senior citizens in that community safe and secure.

She then turned around and told the other three deputies that these were the dirty low-down animals who have been ripping off old men and women in the Village. Several of the residents woke up and saw the 'Cat' *burglars* and almost had heart attacks.

This is exactly why Charlie and all sheriff's *and* cop's say there is no such thing as a 'routine' traffic stop!

Charlie and his A-Team of top flight investigators, was able with the assistance of the CIA (The Agency) to discover that the egregious 'cat burglaries' were committed by the quite infamous "*Flaming Sword*" gang.

The five members of the very dangerous robbers were:

1. Mr. Usman dan Buhari, he was the notorious and ruthless ring leader.

2. Ms. Yemi Mullammadu Saraki, who was the reputed Mata-Hari of Nigeria.

3. Mr. Bukola Fodio Osinbajo, who had big hands and even bigger mouth.

4. Mr. Yakubu Nigeria Omnoghen, was an expert in several martial arts disciplines.

5. Mr. P. W. Nkamu Dogara, wherever he went 'death and gloom' followed him.

Case number three:

"A Kidnapping in Laguna Woods" once again, and to no bodies surprise, occurred in place that the late and great builder and visionary Ross Cortese built. Sarge interrupted Charlie and asked, "Hefa, who is Ross Cortese?"

To which Charlie replied, "I will tell you later, Sarge, but let it suffice for now for me to say he was one of the most important and successful home builders in California as well as the United States, from the 1960's through the 1990s."

The LMS, Inc. corporate officers who call Charlie and requested his assistance, once again, were Betty the outstanding and extremely sharp C.F.O. of the Village and Diane equally bright and sharp financial board member of the Woods in charge of the multi-million dollar budget that the Woods had as their yearly budget from the funds generated by the HOA fees.

This subject criminal case involved the kidnapping of wealthy and famous Laguna Woods Village owners and residents. Charlie told Sarge, the investigation was called, "A Kidnapping in Laguna Woods."

Charlie told Sarge that the name of the innocent kidnapping was, "Marianne Campbell-Smith" who was a very well- liked and quite successful business woman who had previously lived in the breathtaking city of Laguna Beach, California for many years.

That was before Ms. Campbell-Smith retired and moved lovely Laguna Woods, which is just over the hill and only ten minutes away from all of her close personal friends and family in Laguna Beach.

She was married to the quite well known and excellent businessman, "Morton James Irvine Smith." He also was formerly from Laguna Beach and owned several businesses and buildings located there.

Mr. Morton Smith was one of the sons of *"Athalie Anita 'Joan' Irvine Smith*. Joan Irvine Smith is one of the most famous, wealthiest as well as most generous and visible *philanthropists* in all of Orange County, and also the whole United States.

Charlie it just so happens, had actually met the lovely and brilliant Joan Irvine back in the day (1979). He was working for the LAPD (Los Angeles Police Department) at that time and did some 'moonlighting' for some extra pocket money.

Ms. Joan, as Charlie called her, hired several body guards to protect her 24/7 after the very heavily reported kidnapping of several very famous and wealthy people. Namely: a) "Francis (Frank) Albert *Sinatra*, Junior", Franks son, b) "John Paul *Getty* III", the grandson of "J. Paul *Getty*", one of the wealthiest people in the world at that time.

And also, c) 'Aldo *Moro'* the former Prime Minister of Italy, d) "Patricia 'Patty' *Hurst*" she was the granddaughter of "*William Randolph Hurst*" the famous newspaper baron and also one of the richest individuals in the world.

And last, however, certainly not the only famous and/or wealthy person to be kidnapped, was, e) "Adam *Walsh*" son of the quite well known *"John Walsh"* who did the TV show, "America's Most Wanted" still in syndication, even today.

Charlie used to watch that great true criminal investigation show, with his sons every week when his kids were young. Charlie really likes John Walsh, he really does.

Later on, Charlie and his A-Team of investigators, discovered that the *"Red Army Fraction"* a German far-left militant organization had perpetrated the heinous kidnapping of Ms. Campbell-Smith.

They had done this (and also other) kidnapping apparently to raise money for their insurrection and criminal activities in Germany and also in Europe.

Charlie and Sarge, were waiting for an *encrypted* cell phone call from the OCSD Don Barnes, Sheriff and Chief Coroner for all of Orange County and Sarge's boss. The Sheriff works very hard to protect the citizens of the O.C. homes, their businesses, vehicles and residences.

Also, he was highly recommended for his new role as Sheriff by the outstanding former Sheriff, *Sandra Hutchens* as well as 17 local police chiefs. And he was following the 'Shootings in Laguna Woods' very carefully.

The 'New Sheriff-in-town' was a hand's on type of law enforcement officer. He told his large staff to keep him informed of any criminal activity that affected, women, children, and also the less fortunate people of his (Orange) County.

While waiting for the Sheriff to call back, for he is an extremely busy man, Charlie open a *Christian* book that he was reading and said to Sarge his sidekick and best friend, "Sarge did you know this stuff." To which the Sarge replied, "What stuff, Charlie, you are always talking about all kinds of stuff, how am I supposed to know which stuff you are referring too?"

Then Charlie said, "The *fifteen* key points that are listed in the OC Sheriff's Department Training Guide, of course." After which, and before Sarge could reply, our man Charlie started to read the following highlights (summary) from his training guide that he always kept in his beloved BMW glove box. And the following is what he read to Sarge...

CHAPTER TWELVE

THEN CHARLIE PROCEEDED to tell Sarge about the Deputy, Police Officer, and PI, study guide that he had in his BMW glove box. By the way, everybody who knows Charlie, knows that he absolutely loves BMW cars. He truly does.

He always tells anyone who will listen, "The BMW is the ultimate driving machine and that it is one of the finest road production vehicles in the world." Also, that, "they never wear out, and they last almost forever if you take good care of them."

Sarge responded by saying, "Charlie, old man, I like BMW as well, but you cannot beat a Chevy, if you ask me." And then added, "I always say go Chevy V-8 or go home."

Then Sarge laughed and laughed again, then continued his diatribe with Charlie, "I will race your BMW 840-M class with my new Chevy Camaro with a 454 HP high output V-8 engine with racing suspension any day of the week."

Charlie replied very quickly, "OK Sarge, I accept your challenge, let's take our cars out to the 'LA County Fair Grounds' in Pomona, California and see which car win in a quarter-mile course that they have out there that you can rent for a safe and sane vehicle race on a closed tract."

So, then they both drove out the Santa Ana Freeway (5) to the 241 Fast Track Expressway then to the 91 (Riverside Freeway) to the 71 Ontario Freeway until they got to the 10 (San Bernardino) Freeway.

They paid the $500.00 standard race course fee, and had at it. Charlie won, but by just a few seconds. It was almost a dead tie. However, Sarge said that he had won and Charlie told him "In your dreams."

When they returned to Laguna Woods Village for the investigation, but before they resumed it, Charlie pulled out the Scripture Study guide, once again, and said to Sarge, "Here this is the quite important stuff that I was telling you about before my BMW beat your Chevy Camaro."

Then he added, "And Sarge, please pay close attention, as this is very important stuff, alright?" Sarge, just smiled, and nodded his head that he was listening to his Hefa and best friend."

And the following is what Charlie read to Sarge from the short but very powerful and informative Deputy Study guide which was totally based upon the experiences and real-life cases of the OCSD and the Law Enforcement Officers in the O.C.

Fifteen Key Points from the OCSD Guide:

1. You are quite fortunate to be a big part of the OCSD. Your employment at the OCSD was not an accident. You were predestined to be here. Be proud of that.

2. You are to be completely blameless, loyal and also devoted to your local OC citizens. This means that you are fit to serve them, despite any shortcomings.

3. You are to care for the less fortunate people, as well as all women and children. In Orange County, and also, to be as decent a person as you can be.

4. You are here now, and you shall remain here until you retire. This is not just a job this is your *Career*. You are now part of a big, very big family, the OCSD family. The OCSD has selected you to be their very own sons and daughters. or son.

5. You were selected by the OCSD for your own personal, individual as well as unique abilities. And, you have many least you forget.

6. You will be required, on a regular basis, to give your sweat, tears and even your blood, perhaps, to serve and protect your OC community.

7. You have made a serious commitment to have great personal integrity, including but not limited to forgiving yourselves for

any wrongs that you have done in your past, which in your own mind, you feel are unpardonable. [Please see, I John 1:9].

8. You have the plentiful resources of the OCSD. They have all of the help and assistance that you will ever need to do your job with the best of your personal abilities and strengths. You have 'unmerited favor' from your fellow brothers and sisters of the OCSD.

*****

9. You have been allowed to have the OCSD mysteries and successes and history known to you, unlike anyone else in Orange County. You, even in this crazy, faulty world of war, suffering, evil doers, disease, this world where 'bad things' happen to good people, all too frequently, your devotion to duty, and your life (perhaps) will be required.

10. You have obtained your lifelong personal goal, and at great personal sacrifice and effort. Now you can wipe away every tear from your eyes, and you will no longer have any pain nor sorrow. Also, there will be no more hurt, pain, because all former things of these kinds are no gone, forever."

11. You have found the true way to serve and protect the general public in the OC and you will do just that with your every breath. You will also protect and back-up your fellow OC Law Enforcement officers.

12. You have the promise of the OCSD to be there for you when you need help and/or assistance, of any kind, any kind whatsoever.

You are a light into the OC's (sometimes) world of darkness. You are, however, not without guidance or assistance. You have been thoroughly trained, and prepared, and you have heard the good news about the good and great, OCSD.

13. You know the hope of our wonderful Orange County, California. Your calling over your life is the basket you can put all of your eggs in, so to speak. It is an anchor for your personal and professional life. It is a solid rock and it will never end in vain, never, ever.

14. You are the riches of the OCSD, you are its inheritance and you also are its future. You will receive an eternal reward for your sacrifices, pain and suffering. You really will.

15. You have been given the great personal responsibility to do for the honest, and tax paying citizens of the OC, to protect them when and if they need help. And in any manner that you are able to do so.

When Charlie was done reading the brief 'summary' of this absolutely informative book from the OCSD, Sarge said, "Charlie that was great, and yes I did know some of those fifteen *key points from the OCSD training manual,* but not all of them, so thank you very much my friend for sharing them with me."

The Charlie said to Sarge, "I wonder why it is taking the Sheriff so long to get back to us?" And then Sarge responded, "While you were reading old man, very slowly if I may say so, a high school kid can read (and spell) better than you can, anyway, I got a text from the Sheriff and he was busy helping out at a battered woman's shelter in Orange."

Charlie said, very heatedly at first, but then caught himself, and laughed, "Very funny Sarge. At least when I shoot at the bullseye target at the OCSD firing range, I hit all my shots in center-mass and you get one out of seven in the center and all of the other six around the edges."

Then they both had a big belly laugh at each other and then Charlie spoke, "Alright enough levity, let's call the Sheriff back and then let's go solve this crime, OK Sarge?" And Sarge, who was still laughing at his own funny joke about Charlie, said, "Yes, Charlie let's do this."

And, then Sarge added, he always had to have the last word with his Hefa, Charlie, "Just remember, you may be Sonny Crockett but I *am* Ricco Tubbs."

CHAPTER THIRTEEN

CHARLIE AND SARGE, his ever-present and very loyal investigator, and BBF (best friend forever), who was on loan from the great Orange County Sheriff's Department and the very dedicated OCSD Sheriff himself (Don Barnes), now finally knew, without a *shadow* of doubt, who the 'dirty' low down snake-in-the-grass that tried to murder them both in 'cold blood' was.

Now, and finally after a lot of hard work and a quite lengthy and involved investigation by the Orange County Sherriff Department (*Sheriff Don Barnes*), the Orange County District Attorney (*Todd Spitzer*), the FBI local office in Los Angeles.

The 'Agency' (CIA) in Langley, Virginia, OCSD Community Policing (*Captain Danks*), OCSD Southwest Captain (*Jeffrey Puckett*), and Jan Smoker, of course, with his terrific, fearless and loyal sidekick, Sarge.

The mysterious and vicarious "*Shooting in Laguna Woods*" has been solved. And, also at the same time Charlie and Sarge figured out who had tried to 'ambush' them at '666' Calle Aragon in Laguna Woods Village (which was just as important to them as was the '*Shooting*' case.

Then Charlie said to Sarge, "You know my *niño*, one of my favorite verses is Philippians 4:6-7." And then he encouraged Sarge to read it as soon as he had free some time."

Sarge took the Deputy manual, that Charlie's handed him and read the great verses out loud, "Be anxious (do not worry , and do not fret and have no *fear*) for nothing, but in all things with requests, let the words of your mouth and the meditation of your heart be acceptable in the sight of the honest and law abiding citizens of Orange County, California as well as everywhere in our nation."

Sarge said just as soon as he read the be 'safe and sound' suggestions, "I like what the *manual* said, Charlie. We have very dangerous and life-threatening jobs and vocations and it is very reassuring to know that we nothing to Fear, but Fear itself."

Then he went on to say, "I worry too much sometimes old man, and fret as well. Now I realized that I should be reading more for more 'courage' and strength instead of being so anxious and fearful."

Charlie responded very quickly, "That's right *amigo*, the more I myself research, the less I worry and fret. There is nothing that the heinous crooks and criminals, of this crazy old mixed up OC and the world, can do to us, nothing at all, they cannot hurt us in anyway."

Then Charlie got a call from the OCSD Sheriff, *Don Barnes*, who told Sarge and Charlie that, "The dirty low-down scoundrel who had tried, and tried real-hard, to put both Sarge and Charlie six feet underneath a lovely hand carved headstone made out of granite.

The Sheriff took a breath, and then continued his findings to Sarge, "The 'bad actor' was a security guard in the Village and also was a former attorney. I do not like attorneys normally, but there are exceptions. For example, we have a lot of outstanding attorneys who work in our OCDA office in Santa Ana."

When taken into custody by the OCSD Southwest Division *Captain Jeffrey Puckett*, sang like a canary. He told the Captain that he had been hired by a woman for a hit (killing) contract on our old beloved Charlie and Sarge.

This woman, that hired the hit man, they later found out, was named unknown but whose fellow criminals called by her alias, "*Cat Woman*". She was said to be very crafty, attractive but in a deadly way and extremely dangerous.

When the OCDA (Orange County District Attorney) checked out a woman criminal, with that same *moniker* background, he found out that she was known to be exceptionally anti-*OCSD* and opposed to all law *enforcement* in general.

Also, the *OCDA* said that she absolutely hated PI's (Private Investigators) like 'Charlie' for example. She supposedly did not appreciate ‘private detective’s’ poking around in (her) Village business.

Charlie then said to Sarge, “If it kills me, and it very well might, I am going to find out who the “Cat Woman” is. And when I do find out, I am going to get my retribution against her for trying to kill Sarge and I.”

Sarge replied, *“Hefa*, you go and I will back you up 100%. And you can take that to the bank.”

“To be continued”.

EPILOGUE

ONE OF OUR man Charlie's favorite sayings, since he is a real PI (private investigator) is, "Look at the *birds* of the air, they do not sow nor reap or store away in barns, and yet they are always feed."

And the man up-stairs, looks down and protects and cares for old Charlie, in every way and every day in his quite dangerous line of work. PI's get shot, stabbed and/or killed, all the time in the United States as well as around the globe.

Charlie likes to say, "We are going to have many difficulties in our human lives, 'trials and tribulations' he always calls them here in this crazy old mixed up world, but what we are supposed to do, at the very least, is to try to meet them head-on, *persevere*, have courage, be patient, and keep on fighting the good fight."

Yes, it is hard to do, however, trying to ignore them and/or go around them because you feel that would be easier, is not the right choice, not at all. And you and I can turn our 'disadvantages' into 'advantages' in our personal as well as our business lives.

Finally, Charlie lives by two main rules of engagement in his professional life, 1) A man should do what he says that he is going to do, and, 2) If he does not do what he said that he was going to do, he should be held 'accountable' for his actions.

And then in a heat-beat, or just about 60 seconds in real-time, our favorite PI (private detective), Charles 'Charlie' Warner Kennedy O'Brien, the fine Irish lad that he is, was *gone*, just gone for *now*, but he will *'be-back'* just as Arnold Schwarzenegger (the famous motion picture A-Listed actor, and former Governor of great State of California) always says in his action movies!

Watch *your back* out there Charlie, ole man, and the wind at you back, God's speed and safety!

REDUX

Now, back to this great song was written, Charlie told Sarge, by Phil Collins and Hugh Padgham in 1981. It was picked to open the *Miami Vice* TV show when it started in 1984. The song was said to be one of the greatest (101 on the famous list) of the greatest 'drumming moments' in pop music history.

Also, it was listed as being one of the 100 greatest songs of the 1980s.

"In the Air tonight"

"I can feel it coming in the air tonight, oh Lord, and I've been waiting for this moment for all my life, oh Lord, can you feel it coming in the air tonight? Oh Lord, oh Lord!

Well, I remember, I remember don't worry. How could I ever forget? It's the first time, the first time, the last time we ever met. But I know the reason why you keep your silence up.

No, you don't fool me. Well, the hurt doesn't slow, but the pain still grows. It's no stranger to you or me!"

(Written by Phil Collins and Hugh Padgham. Published 1981).